Still, At Your Door:

A Fictional Memoir

To My favorite Memoirist,

Emma Ramos

Emma Eden Ramos

Still, At Your Door: A Fictional Memoir
by Emma Eden Ramos

Still, At Your Door: A Fictional Memoir is a work of fiction. Names, characters, places, and incidents are either the product of the author's imagination or are used fictitiously. Any resemblance to actual persons, living or dead, business establishments, events or locales is entirely coincidental.

Poetry by Emily Dickinson accessed via Project Gutenberg's Poems: Three Series, Complete, by Emily Dickinson, published for fair use in 2004 by Jim Tinsley.

ISBN: 978-1-927044-94-0
ISBN-10: 1927044944

"*Still, At Your Door: A Fictional Memoir* is a very real, very fluid lesson in life, in abuse, the dynamics of power, of sex and the relationships between people. In this book, Author Emma Eden Ramos brings forth both the bitter and the sweet on wings of articulate, elegant prose, delivering a read that is as deep and wise as it is gripping and powerful."

~ E.S. Wynn, Author of the *Pink Carbide* series, Chief Editor at Thunderune Publishing, *Daily Love Journal* and *Yesteryear Fiction Magazine.*

"*Still, At Your Door: A Fictional Memoir* is a power-house of emotion from the moment you begin. Sabrina Gibbons' story is upended from the moment her mother drags them out of their abusive home in Butler, Penn, and drops them off with their grandparents in the Big Apple. Like New York City, this novella precariously teeters between nightmares and dreams, exploring mutual dependence where one wrong step over the threshold can lead to disaster."

~ Serena M. Agusto-Cox, Reviewer at *Savvy Verse & Wit* and *War Through the Generations.*

Emma Eden Ramos

DEDICATION

In memory of Atticus
AMICI OPTIMI IN AETERNUM

.

my pilgrim soul rings for release.
i will not *forsake*
the aim of my blooming.

Brooke Elise Axtell, "playing savior"

Jagged

I hold tight to my memories of the solid years. Each one is a crystal vase filled to the brim with brightly colored petals. Summer, '99: Missy is five, I'm six. We're vacationing at Virginia Beach with Mom and Dad. Mom wears a black one-piece, a white sun hat and no sunscreen. Her lanky, bronzed legs shimmer under the fiery rays, but it's all well and good. "Gypsy skin," she explains, lathering up my little sister. "You and I have it." She winks at me. "Missy here's more like Daddy." In front of us, Dad talks to a blonde boy with a surfboard. He turns to us and beckons. I jump to my feet, eager to hit the waves. "Sabrina." Mom presses her leathery palms against my cheeks. "Bri-bear." She kisses my nose. "Go on." I grab Missy's hand and we scamper toward the giant salt pond, ready for Dad to scoop us up and wade us through.

Another summer, many years later, Missy and I come across what looks like a secret stash of sea glass. We collect the emerald green fragments just as a mother-sized wave unfurls to scoop them back up. The edges have been smoothed over, calmed. I slide my index finger across one side of the largest piece. Missy stands next to me, peering out toward the horizon. I turn to her, the glass held tightly in my fist. Before I can begin, she says, "Water life is easier."

"Huh?" I stare down at the rushing waves. A thick clump of seaweed tickles my ankle.

Missy seizes a shard from her stash and flings it. The water swallows the glass whole. There's no resistance on either side. "It wasn't ready." She shakes her head.

"What does that mean?" I ask. "How is water life easier?"

"I don't know. I guess… you go in jagged. You're jagged when you go in but smooth when you come out."

Trying to understand, I scrutinize my sister's profile. I recognize our mother in her pronounced cheekbones, her long black lashes.

"But not us." Missy speaks to the open water. I just happen to be standing by. "We come in soft, without edges. Those come later."

"You mean we get jagged with age?"

"Yes." Missy's eyes grow big. She cocks her head to one side, then turns to meet my gaze. "That's what happens to us."

Chapter One

From our second floor bedroom, I hear the old red Ford sputter. *Brrr, brrr, brrr.* The brief silence is followed by a *clang* and a *fuck!*

"What the hell?" Missy's bed creaks. "What's going on?"

My bed is closest to the window. I get up and tiptoe over. "Shush," I whisper. "You'll wake Gracie." Looking back, I see my little half-sister sprawled over her sheets, her thin brown hair dangling in front of her face. She'll be eight in a little over a week.

Outside, the young January frost stings at our tiny four-paned window. By March the glass will be splattered with white grime, and no one will bother to clean it. Mom's car wheezes thick puffs of smoke, but she is nowhere in sight. I search for her, notice Jim's truck is gone from its spot, then jump, startled as the front door slams, its metal chimes making a racket against the wood and glass.

"Huh?" Grace sits up, wide-eyed. "What's wrong?"

As I head over to Grace's bed, the sound of Mom's heels rattle up the stairs and through the rickety hallway. All three of us freeze, waiting for her to reach our door.

"Come on! Come on!" Bursting into the bedroom, two packed pocketbooks slung over one shoulder, Mom fumbles around for the light switch. I shudder as the bulb flicks the room into candescent disruption. The fluorescent glare gives her a grotesque glow, and I wince at her mismatched outfit, caked-on foundation and crooked maraschino-cherry-red lipstick. She jerks from one side to the other, as though trying to latch on to some invisible thought strand. "Come on, girls," she manages, before rushing to the window. "Get up. Get! Goodness, how did I produce such lazy... let me open this window. It's New York time. Get your clothes on. The car has to... no time for breakfast. Let's go!"

"What?" Missy and I start at once. Grace just stares blankly, her mouth hung open like an untended puppet's.

"We're going to New York, Babies!" Mom dances across the room, smiling. I notice a dark ring under her eye. The purple skin pokes out beneath a thick layer of pale foundation.

"Where's Jim?" I turn to Grace. Her knees pressed against her forehead, she rocks back and forth, whispering something I can't make out.

"The bus leaves in an hour." Mom jiggles the almost unhinged doorknob before exiting. "We're done with this place for good."

As the door slams shut, I whirl around on the balls of my feet. The floor resists my calloused pads, firing splinters into the softer areas of my toes. Missy meets my stare with a scowl. "Fuck this shit!" she snaps, tossing her sheets to the floor. I don't respond because there is nothing to say. It's been a while, but we've made this move before. Sure, the details vary slightly each time, but we've got the gist down pat: four sets of clothes each, Grace's stuffed dolphin she calls Daisy Girl, toiletries, a few books, my ten-year-old denim knapsack and my new journal with the words *The Sky's the Limit* written in cursive on the cover. Missy grumbles, stepping into her jeans from the day before.

"Will we have *real* school in New York?" Grace stands next to me, two fingers lodged between her lips.

"Yes," I nod, stopping to yank her hand from her mouth. "You wanna look like a rabbit when you're my age?"

She pulls Daisy Girl from the pile I've arranged on the floor. "No." She hugs the stuffed animal to her chest. "We'll actually go there? To school?"

"Uh-huh. Remember?" It's true. In New York City, when we stay with Grandma Marta and Grandpa Kal, school is not Mom gathering us into the kitchen at midnight to help her learn the lines to a play she hopes to star in some day. It isn't me yelling at Missy because she's filled out Grace's state administered home exam in her own fifteen-year-old handwriting. School, when we live with Grandma Marta and Grandpa Kal, is that place we go and, for six hours each day, pretend that we are normal girls… girls who know very ordinary lives.

~~~~

The engine rumbles beneath us as we say goodbye to the gray ramshackle we've come to accept as our home. Grace taps her fingernail against the chilled car window. She blows warm breath on the glass and, before the moisture can evaporate, draws a tiny heart with a smiley face in the middle. Missy sits with her legs up, her forehead pressed against her knees, the music from her headphones competing with the asthmatic car engine.

"Mom?" I whisper, reaching across the cup holder where an opened twenty-four ounce can of beer has been sitting for almost a month. As I brush Mom's cheek, sticky residue from her foundation sinks between the cracks on my index finger.

She turns to me and smiles. "Yes, Bear?" I see she is only ten miles above the speed limit.

"What do you want me to tell Grandma and Grandpa?"

"About what?" Her eyes are level with mine, but I know she isn't really looking *at* me. I'm more like a blank screen, something stable and empty for her to project on to. Once again, I point to the purple ring under her eye.

"Oh." She pauses and, for a moment, reverts back to the road. "Remember when I played Blanche? You remember, in *A Streetcar Named Desire*, back when we lived in Roanoke."

"Yes," I nod. "I remember."

"Grandma and Grandpa came to see me then. They sat with you and Missy right up there in the front row." Tilting her head back, Mom shuts her eyes as if to hold the memory still: keep it in present time. "Your daddy carried Missy backstage afterwards. I don't know if she ever got to see my final fight with Stanley, but you, Bear, you stayed awake for the whole show! That's why we're going to New York now." Mom takes hold of my hand, her bony fingers disappearing into the spaces between mine. I try not to flinch as the tips of her nails dig into my palm. "All we need's a little time and money, Bri." She pauses, then swivels, looking back at Grace and Missy. Both have dozed off. "Time and money."

Feet up on the dashboard, I take my journal out from my beat-up knapsack. I'm fifty pages into this one already – fifty pages of thoughts, hopes, stories, some real, some made up. *New York*, I write in sprawling letters. *New beginnings?*

Chapter Two

Stocky and graceless, the bus rattles through the heart of Pennsylvania. For a short while I imagine we are in an above-ground submarine, studying the rapidly changing landscape. There, to my right, that neon blue racecar is the Great White of the highway. Step in its path and you'll be smashed to pulp and bone. Those small houses on the edge of our path? They're nooks, crevices in the residential coral reef. The further you venture into the reef, the larger, safer they become. But as outsiders, fast moving spectators in this above ground marine system, we don't get to enjoy the comforts of those areas. We're simply passing through.

After four hours of side-to-side rocking with the occasional sharp turn or jolting stop, nausea makes it difficult to imagine anything pleasant. Missy's listened to her music until the power ran low. Now she's off, complaining to me about the guy in front of us who smells like he hasn't showered since last month. Mom, she says, is at the back of the bus, emptying her pouch of single shot Vodka bottles while flirting with a group of college-aged boys. Grace is happy to sit and watch, giggling when Mom speaks in funny accents and does impersonations.

"I think she's disgusting," Missy snarls as the sound of Mom's laugh infiltrates the otherwise undisturbed space.

"She isn't hurting anyone." I cradle my stomach, trying to keep it as still as possible. We haven't eaten since last night and I realize, if I shut my eyes and focus real hard, I can almost smell the cinnamon French toast Mom made on Sundays back when Dad was around.

"Why are we going this time, anyway?" Missy shakes me from my daydream. "I mean, we haven't even seen Grandma and Grandpa in over a year."

"Did you see Mom's eye?" It's moments like this that I hate my sister.

"So?" Missy shrugs. "If we left home every time Jim hit Mom we—"

"Jim's a bastard."

"Mom's a freak!"

"Damn, Marissa!" Before I can stop myself, I shove her. Grabbing hold of the armrest, Missy catches herself from falling into the aisle.

"Don't touch me!" She socks me in the bicep. "Don't ever fucking touch me."

Blinking hard, I turn to face the window. I steady my breathing and clench my fists.

"Hey," Missy shakes my shoulder. "Hey, sorry."

"Don't worry about it," I whisper.

"Did I hurt you?"

"No."

Forehead pressed against the window, I shut my

eyes and, hugging my empty stomach, give way to the lulling of the engine. My mind, rotating like an old rolodex, pauses, latches on, then holds still to the image of that big theater in Virginia.

The seats are dark red velvet. I can smell the musky scent of old shoes and stale snacks. Staring at the crowd behind me, I run my chubby, six-year-old hand up and down the back of my chair. I like the way the material defies every other stroke, turning a deeper shade as it resists being smoothed in the opposite direction. Do they notice us sitting here in the front row? I wonder – all those theater old-timers, as Mom calls them. Grandma and Grandpa sit cross-legged, whispering to each other in that language from the country with the funny name. Hungary: I imagine a town of men, women and children sitting around, waiting for their dinners. "It's spelled Hun-gary," Grandma Marta explained. "Not hungry." I still think it's a silly name for a place to be from.

Missy jiggles in her seat. "I gotta go again," she whispers. Dad and I exchange glances. "Oh, yeah. This time I got both in there," she giggles, pointing to her belly. "Number one and—"

"Alright, we get the picture." Dad scoops Missy up. "Sabrina," he rustles my hair. "Three minutes, tops."

I nod, turning around to face the stage. Extending my arm, I bend forward and stroke the splintery edge. I imagine Mom waiting in the wings and try to tune out the chatter around me to see if I can hear her. Maybe she's practicing, rehearsing that scene she loves when the 'horrid' doctors come to take Blanche away. I hate that part, but Mom's told me about a hundred times. "It's just part of the play, Bear. When you see me on stage, you must remember that. It's a part I'm playing. It isn't real."

The theater lights grow dim, and Dad rushes to our row, Missy tucked over his shoulder. "Phew!" He sighs. "That was a close one."

I clench my fists, trying not to wiggle with excitement as the stage lights shoot out from the high ceiling. Piano music begins, and two women cross to the middle of the stage.

"Where's Mom?" Missy whispers.

"Shh!" I hiss.

Two men appear and the play begins. Growing restless, I catch myself kicking the bottom of the stage. Grandma Marta grabs hold of my leg. Leaning over, I brush the edge with my index finger then look up. Her beige heels announce her arrival. Dressed all in white, she reminds me of a prima ballerina – straight and steady, yet delicate at the same time. That's my mom! I want to shout so every person in the theater can hear. That is MY mom—

"Hey!" Grace leans over me, patting the top of my head. "Wake up, sleepy!"

I open my eyes, one side of my face smushed against the dirty bus window. *There's the rush!* The scene outside sends a pulse from the top of my head to the bottoms of my feet. Skyscrapers: imposing or protecting, depending on how you look at them. Like mountains or tidal waves, they tower ominously, reminding you just how tiny you are – tiny but safe, at least momentarily, if the sky should fall. Cars exhibiting the entire range of the color spectrum ripple forward, coming to a halt every few seconds. The cluster of serious faces, smoke from sidewalk pretzel carts: New York City!

"We're here." Grace hugs my neck. "Finally!"

I press my palms against her smooth, grinning cheeks.

~ ~ ~ ~

"In, in!" Mom hustles Missy and Grace into the taxi. I shove our duffle bag in the jaws of the trunk then stop. "Mom, your stuff! Where's your suitcase?" Searching frantically, I realize I hadn't seen her with anything besides two pocket books when we left Butler. "You forgot to bring—"

"I have everything I need." Facing in the opposite direction, Mom fidgets with the cab door handle. "I'll get some new things later, Bear." She turns to me, sporting a half smile, her eyes cool and calm. "Come on."

We speed through the streets of Manhattan, Grace wiggling in her spot between Missy and me. "You missed the ocean, Bri! It was huge, like this big!" She stretches her arms out wide. "Missy said not to wake you up, but I wanted to show you when we went over the bridge."

"It's a river," Missy corrects. "Just a dirty river, filled with garbage and—"

"Stop!" Mom yells as we approach the red brick building with its long, dark green awning. The driver hits the brakes, and I throw my arm out, catching Grace from knocking her head against the seat divider.

"Jesus, Lady!" The driver brings his fist down on his steering wheel.

Mom flings her passenger door open. Tossing a mixture of bills and loose change in the man's lap, she motions for me to hurry. I climb out, turning back to take Grace's hand. Looking up, I notice the driver staring wide-eyed, his gaze level with mine. He mumbles something I can't make out, turns to Missy, then Grace. "Jee-sus." He shakes his head.

"Come on." I grab Grace's hand, helping her out of the car.

Lined up like three still-standing bowling pins, Missy, Grace and I watch the taxi roll off into the Upper West Side. "That guy was weird." Grace tugs at my coat. "Why'd he say Je—?"

"Oh, shit!" Mom claps her hands together. "Oh!" Standing in front of us, she clasps Missy's and my arms, forming a tight huddle. "You know what? Damn it! I... you three go up to the apartment. I need to do something."

"What?" Missy grumbles. "It's freezing out here!"

"I know. I forgot... Babies, you go up, okay?"

Taking Grace's hand, Missy starts toward the building, leaving me to tend to our belongings.

"Mom?" I sling our duffle bag over my shoulder. My knees buckle under the weight, but I steady my footing. "I'll come with you."

"No, Bear." She strokes my chilled cheek with her bony knuckles. I close my eyes and, for a split second, see the glistening Virginia Beach water ripple toward me like a mirage.

"Go, help your sisters." Mom's chin quivers as she catches her breath, coughs, then smiles, looking down at the pavement. "Go on."

"How long?" I turn, unable to resist the beckoning warmth of the apartment building's lobby.

"Minutes, Bear!" Mom's voice trails off. "Minutes."

Chapter Three

Sheila! Sheila!

I jolt awake, the memory of Grandma Marta running to the building stairwell, calling for my mother, still ringing in my head. Rubbing my eyes, I turn to the bedside alarm. *6:30 AM, Thursday, January 13.* Almost seven days, but still no word. The landline back home in Butler is cut off. Mom stopped paying her cell phone bill months ago, so there's nothing to do but wait. I slip out of bed, trying to make as little noise as possible, then remember it's only me. In Mom's old room with the pictures of olden-day movie stars, Greta Garbo and Vivien Leigh, and that giant poster of Audrey Hepburn in *Sabrina*, the movie for which I am named, I'm alone.

The newly tiled floor keeps still as I tiptoe past the adjacent rooms with my sleeping sisters, and toward the kitchen. Grandma and Grandpa's voices mingle with the sound of a whistling teakettle. I park myself outside the kitchen doors, knowing full well they'll go into Hungarian if they think I'm up and listening.

"Kalman," Grandma speaks in her sharp, almost masculine voice. "I'm going to the police station after I get the girls to school this morning."

"No, come on. We'll give her some time."

"Time? Kal, she's sick! She's a sick woman with three children, and—" Grandma switches to a whisper. "That pig husband has her drinking again."

"You don't know that. How do you know—?"

"Marissa told me."

I look back down the hallway at the room Missy's staying in. I could strangle her!

"Okay, so what are the police going to do? Huh?" Grandpa clears his throat. "A forty-five year old grown woman decides to drop her kids at her parents and—"

"No. She's disturbed, and she's *never* done this before. Just leaving them here with no word, nothing! Please. If we can find her, maybe we can get her into some place where—"

"No!" Grandpa brings his thick fist down on the oak table. I put my hands over my mouth to keep from gasping. "Not again! I'm telling you no."

"Be reasonable, Kal. We can't all just wait until—"

"I said no and that's final!"

I jump, a door creaking behind me. Wheeling around, I shuffle to Uncle Victor's old bedroom. Grace stands in the doorway, Daisy Girl tucked under her arm. "Did Mom come yet?" She rubs her eyes, following me back into the room Missy and I stayed in the last time we came to live with Grandma and Grandpa. Mom stayed in her old bedroom.

"No," I whisper, flipping the light switch. "Not yet."

"But she will come for my birthday." Grace settles,

cross-legged on the bed with its puffy blue spread. She nods, holding Daisy Girl at arms length. "She'll come then."

Grandma and Grandpa stop arguing as Grace and I make our way into the kitchen. Grace sets Daisy Girl in the middle of the breakfast table then scurries to the cereal cabinet.

Standing ballerina-straight, Grandma folds her arms, watching Grace rummage. "Can you tell Grandpa how many bowls of soup you ate last night?"

"Almost four." Grace turns to Grandpa. "Three and a half, maybe."

"Three and a half." Grandma nods, tossing a fierce glance at Grandpa. "Does Momma cook for you at home?" She runs her long fingers through Grace's hair.

"She—" I begin.

"I didn't ask you," Grandma snaps.

Grace looks up at me, then at Grandma. She shrugs, sticking her middle and index fingers in her mouth.

"It's like we need the Soviet Union to come in for private interrogations with you girls." Grandma walks over to the piping teakettle. "Sabrina, sit down please."

"I'm fine here." With my back against the door, I stare down at my hands. I close my eyes, and brush the backs of my fingers against my cheek. *Minutes, Bear*, I hear Mom call out. *Minutes*. I imagine her somewhere close by, maybe staying in a cheap hotel while she looks for acting work and a place to live. She will come for us; that much I know. As long as I can keep Missy and Grace from telling Grandma how things were before we left Butler, everything will be okay. Life can go back to the way it was when Dad was around. Mom will be happy if she's acting. Jim will stay gone. Everything will be alright.

~ ~ ~ ~

"Gracie, your pants!" Missy laughs, shaking her head as we stand, all four of us, waiting for the streetlight to change in our favor.

"What?" Grace stomps, looking down. "They're not bad!"

"They're way too short, but you know what? If our new school floods, you'll be the one kid with dry pants."

I cover my mouth to keep from giggling. Grandma smiles. "Marissa, you would have gotten a real kick out of your mom when she was your age."

"What do you mean?" I ask turning to Missy. I'd like to wipe the grimace off her face.

"Your mom," Grandma begins, leading us across the street, "always had some smart remark. Always. In primary school they said it was a sign of high intelligence."

"Missy is super smart," I agree, grinning at my sister, who I know thinks nothing could be worse than being compared to our mother. "But I think I'm more like Mom." Looking down at my naturally tanned skin and long, skinny limbs, I nod. "At least I look like her."

"No." Grandma stops, her tempered oak eyes softening as she studies me. "You are the spitting image of your father. You really are. You're Tom Gibbons' daughter."

For a split second the sidewalk seems to surge before me. I catch my breath, struggling to keep balance. *Tom Gibbons.* The name is written on the checks Mom collects every month – *Name of deceased: Thomas Gibbons* – but something about hearing it spoken makes me feel limp, as though my bones could turn to liquid, leaving behind a defenseless layer of skin – the skin I share in common with my mother and my mother's mother.

"If my dad is different from Bri and Missy's, does that mean Missy gets to be more of Bri's sister than me?" Grace tugs on Grandma's brown suede coat as we turn the corner, nearing a stone building with giant blue doors and an iron gate enclosing the entrance. Three girls shuffle past. One stops to look at us then continues onward, turning back and whispering in her friend's ear. Following the girls to the front steps of the school, Missy and I swap anxious glances.

"Can we go in separately?" Missy asks, lagging behind. Another group of kids pass by, eyeing Missy and me.

"Don't be ridiculous!" Grandma motions. "We're late as it is. Come."

The long gray hallway leads us through a maze flanked with lockers, brightly painted doors and clusters of faces. Some seem interested in the two teenage girls following the aging woman with the little girl clutching her coat sleeve, two fingers stuck between her lips. Others seem oblivious. I resist the urge to thank each indifferent face we pass: *I appreciate your not caring. Really. You're making this experience just a tad less humiliating. Thank you!*

Hustling us through the Administration Office door, Grandma announces to the man at the front desk, "We're here to see Ms DeSousa. I'm Marta Farkas. Ms

De—"

"Mrs Farkas." A heavy-set woman peers out from behind one of the thin, grey cubicles. "Come right this way."

I reach out for Missy's hand then think better of it. I dig my fists into my coat pockets.

"You must be Sabrina and Marissa Gibbons." Ms DeSousa smiles, squinting behind purple-rimmed bifocals. "Beautiful girls. And you're our new second grader?"

Grace nods, looking down at the floor.

"I'm sorry we're a bit late." Grandma pulls Grace's hand from her mouth.

"Not to worry, Mrs Farkas. Homeroom doesn't end for another fifteen minutes. I'll tell you what; if you'll wait here with the little one," Ms DeSousa winks at Grace, "I'll take your granddaughters to their homerooms where they can get settled. Then we can take care of the paperwork."

Grandma agrees. Missy and I follow Ms DeSousa back into the busy hallway.

Standing to the side, I wait while Ms DeSousa ushers Missy through the paint chipped door with *10B* written below its small square window. I wave as Missy looks back at me. Biting her lower lip, she shakes her head then disappears.

"I'm sorry to hear about your mother. I do hope she recovers soon." Ms DeSousa sighs, leading me down the hall toward the stairwell.

"Huh?" I stop, looking up.

"Oh, perhaps I shouldn't have mentioned it. It's just... well, I want you to know that Whitman Prep is a very supportive place. We have a Wellness Center where you and Marissa are always welcome to stop by just to chat if, you know, there is anything on your mind, and of course, my door is always open."

There's a hole in my shoe. I realize, curling my toes to hold in the tension, that my sand colored sock pokes through the top of my left sneaker. Perhaps the Wellness Center has extra shoes. They may be interested to know that I have a hole in my shoe. Sure, it isn't a big hole but it may grow. If I continue to wiggle my toes, the hole could take over my entire shoe. The people at the Wellness Center, I am sure, would be very happy to chat with me about the soon-to-be monster sized hole in my left shoe.

"Well, here we are." Ms DeSousa pats my shoulder, her other hand placed firmly on the metal door handle. "Eleven D."

Taking a deep breath, I watch the handle tilt ninety degrees then stop. I step through the door and into a brightly lit room with about twenty faces looking my way.

Chapter Four

"Everyone…" The man behind the desk gestures toward me as though I were one of those cars on display at the mall. "This is…" He looks down at a piece of paper in front of him. "Sabrina Gibbons. She is a new addition here. Let's welcome her."

Scanning the faces, I recognize the three girls Missy and I crossed earlier outside. They whisper in the back of the class, eyeing me and grinning. I take a seat in the nearest available desk, letting my knapsack drop. Voices close in like a tight band around my head.

"Ben's party was fuckin wild."

"I heard Kayla got so drunk she—"

"There's this new site run by some college kid. Seriously, he'll write your essays for only—"

Focusing on my breath, I lift my knapsack off the floor and rummage, trying to make it seem like I'm doing something.

"The new chick's kinda hot," I hear someone whisper behind me.

"She'd be really hot if she didn't dress like some homeless grunge kid," a gruffer voice mutters. They snicker.

I place my tattered copy of *Jane Eyre* from our library back in Butler (almost a year overdue) on my lap, and search past scattered pencils, a pack of cinnamon flavored gum, some loose-leaf paper Grandma grabbed before we left in a hurry – "This weekend I'm taking you three school shopping," she promised –until I find what I am looking for. Lifting my journal from my knapsack, I make sure its back cover faces the desks behind me so no one can read and scoff at the message of hope written on the front. As I flip to a blank page, a yellowing sheet falls from between the binding and onto my lap. Turning it over, I feel a tug in that soft, lonely spot between my chest and my stomach. She peers off, almost trance-like. Her lips parted in a subtle smile, she seems to be dreaming with open eyes. A few strands of chestnut colored hair reach from the far side of her face, one ambitious enough to try to brush a small freckle on the left side of her chin. My eyes grow moist as I study the old photograph of Mom standing before a wave-less sea, white puffy clouds relaxed in the distance. *You are the spitting image of your father* – Grandma's words hover in the empty space separating me from the picture. *You're Tom Gibbons' daughter.*

~ ~ ~ ~

"This is the gym." Chelsea, my 'peer tour guide' points to a large court with basketball hoops hung on either side. A group of fifteen or so boys run toward the bleachers, each sporting a yellow jersey. "I suggest not wearing *those*." She eyes my beat-up sneakers. "I mean, unless you don't care. You know, I don't use gym as an excuse to be frumpy, but that's just me."

Forcing a smile, I nod. "Thanks." I wonder if Missy's had her tour yet. Please don't let her guide be anything like mine! Just the thought makes me snicker. *Fifteen-year-old Pennsylvania native Marissa Gibbons knocks classmate's teeth out after classmate insults her wardrobe. Classmate agrees to return to school under one condition: non-frumpy dentures must be crafted specially for gym class.*

Chelsea lifts her hot pink-encased phone from her bag. "No way!" she scoffs, her thumbs moving quickly over the type-pad. "Sorry. Um... so you don't mind if we cut this short, do you?" Eyebrows raised, she cocks her head to one side. "I mean, basically I've shown you the important stuff. You can always just ask someone if you can't find something, you know."

"Okay." I nod, staring into her glassy, blue eyes. *Not much there.*

"Great. So if anyone asks, you'll just say we saw the whole school."

"Yup."

"Thanks, Serena."

"Sabrina," I correct.

"Right. Sorry." Chelsea flips her hair, turning to leave me in front of the school gym. "Oh." She swivels back around. "I don't know if you're one of those theater people, but there's a new theater downstairs in the basement. I'm supposed to tell everyone I tour. It's big and... stuff. You know; if you're into that kinda thing."

Looking down at the floor, I watch Chelsea's heels as she walks off. Taking my copy of *Jane Eyre* from my knapsack, I open to a random page and begin reading. I've read the story three times now, cover to cover, so no matter which page I turn to, I always know where I am. Just one floor below, there's a stage. I imagine it, vast and austere, overlooking rows of empty seats. Is it a wooden stage? What are the seats made of? Book in hand, I allow my thoughts to drift, each buoyed by one steady current. Could *I* be one of those 'theater people?'

~~~~

Standing by the school entrance, Missy scowls as I mosey up to wait by her side. "I hate this place," she sighs, turning from me. Her voice quivers, and I put my hand on her shoulder. She shakes it loose.

"Which classes did you have?"

"Where the hell is Grandma?" She kicks the sidewalk. "This is embar—"

"Come on, come." Hurrying across the street, Grandma holds Grace's hand. Lagging behind, Grace rubs her eyes, her face red and swollen.

"What happened?" I bend down as Grace runs toward us.

Huffing, Grandma storms up to Missy and me. "Your sister has a very interesting vocabulary."

"What did you do?" Missy nudges.

Bursting into a sob, Grace buries her face in my coat. "They made me look stupid!" She bellows. A group of boys pass by, staring at the four of us. I pat Grace's head, trying to ignore their critical glares.

"She doesn't read." Digging through her purse, Grandma pulls out a folded sheet of paper. "Do you two know that?" She looks at Missy, then me. "Eight years old in two days and she can't read."

Turning away, I catch the glance of one of the boys. There are five total. I scan the pack then look back at the one with curious eyes. *Enjoying the show?* I want to yell, but he just stares until one of his friends taps him on the shoulder and they continue down the street.

"What happened?" I smooth Grace's light brown hair.

"I hate stupid school," she sniffles.

"Do you want to tell Sabrina what you called your teacher?" Grandma prods with her branch-like finger.

"Nothing," Grace mumbles.

"Nothing?" Grandma shifts to a whisper. "A..." She looks quickly over each shoulder. "A cunt."

"What!"

Missy snickers.

"This isn't funny!" Grandma snaps.

Missy bends down to Grace's eye level. "Do you even know what that means?"

"It... it's a bad lady; a lady who's mean. Dad says it all the time!" Grace leers at Grandma. "I hate my ugly teacher."

"I don't care! You don't talk to anyone like that... ever." Grandma looks up at me, shaking her head. I shrug, my fingers knuckle deep in my half-sister's fine hair. It's true. Take away expletives, and Jim's verbal exchanges would consist mostly of grunts with, okay, perhaps a few words thrown in. I open my mouth to explain, say something in Grace's defense, when I am brought back to the day before we left Butler.

A bitter chill blows in through the cracked window, hissing with each gust. From the bottom of the staircase, I watch the pane tremble, weakening every time air tunnels through its golf-ball-sized hole. Across the room, Jim sits mesmerized by some show on bounty hunters in Australia. "God damn!" He slaps his thigh. "You see? This is why they don't have crime on the other side of the world. These guys are for real. Damn!"

"That's right," Missy smirks, sitting next to me on the third step. "I think I read somewhere that there has never been a single crime committed in Australia. Must be cus of the bounty hunters."

Taking hold of Missy's hand, I squeeze tight, smiling for the first time in days – probably since Mom's incident at the mall. It's happened again and, as usual, we aren't prepared.

For nearly a decade now, the days of Mom crying non-stop that have become as much an indication of late-November as naked trees and lifeless ponds, are followed by excitement and adventure. Mom gets out of bed one morning and *there she is!* I say to myself, and I know why I love her and why my father drove head-on into the opposing highway lane just thinking of her.

Dressed in skinny jeans, a red v-neck top, and shiny black heels, Mom shuffles in at seven AM singing 'Good Morning' from *Singing in the Rain*. Missy and I are up, laughing over the scene from the night before. Even Jim smiled when, after just one margarita, Mom stood on the bar at Hoopers and sang 'See What the Boys in the Backroom will Have' in her best Marlene Dietrich voice. It's mid-December now and we have about two weeks left. The days will be filled with outings and late nights watching old movies and taking bets on whose 'Give me a viskey and soda; Ginger Ale on the side, and don't be stingy, Baby' is most authentic. We'll never say it, but in this small frame, this cut out, ripple-free pool of time, we are the luckiest three girls on earth.

The flip comes when January's first chill has swept over the state. Ponds keep still under a thin layer of ice; trees steady themselves for the season that tests their resilience, but as our outdoor surroundings hunker down, conserving strength, chaos shimmies in through cracks in our untended interior.

Missy nudges my arm, motioning toward the top of the stairs. Grace's constant tapping has finally paid off. Mom stands in the bedroom doorway, her white nightgown hanging off her bony shoulders. "What?"

"I'm hungry." Grace hugs Daisy Girl to her chest.

Shouts from the TV come to a halt. "You ready to be a mother now?" Jim holds the remote, pointing it at Mom as though it were a wand with the power to command domesticity.

I get up and move to the top of the stairs. Missy remains rooted in her spot.

"Just leave her be," Jim growls, turning back to the TV.

"Come." I take Mom's hand, leading her into the bedroom. Grace shuffles close behind. Jim's clothes are scattered over the floor. Cigarette butts form a small hill under his night table. *Carcinogen Mountain*, I say to myself and try to erase the image of Jim in bed next to my mother, polluting the air while she lays in a stupor from the pills the hospital sent her home with three days earlier.

Resting her head in her hands, Mom sits slouched over at the foot of the bed.

"Are you still sick?" Grace pets her arm, cozying up on the bed.

Turning to Grace, Mom rubs her glazed eyes. "What's my name?"

Grace grins. "Momma." She's the only one who still plays this game.

"No." Mom shakes her head. "Not Momma."

"Mommy," Grace giggles. "Missus Mommy!" She breaks into a laugh.

"Missus Mommy. That's a new one."

Bending forward, the two touch noses.

"Sheila." Mom looks up at me. "Mrs Sheila Gibbons."

"Not anymore," I mumble, turning to face the window. A few light drops splatter the dirty pane.

"Hand me those."

I take the orange container Mom points to from the corner of the windowsill. *Sheila Davenport*, it reads. I tap my fingernail at the name, handing over the bottle. Mom raises her eyebrows.

Dumping all the light blue pills into the palm of her hand, she makes a fist then draws it quickly to her mouth. Springing forward, I reach out to grab her wrist, but before I can, she brings her hand back down.

"That isn't funny!" I shout, covering my face. Missy always says I look like a pug when I cry.

Through my own heaving, I don't hear any movement, but as my mother folds her arms around me, she whispers in my ear. "I'm so sorry, Bear. I didn't mean it. Forgive me! Please forgive me."

Grace pats me from behind. "It's okay, Bri," she sooths. "Mom's not sick anymore. See? She's better now."

Shifting to the present, my back against the gate surrounding our new school, I look down at Grace's tear-stained face. Her searching, cocoon-shaped eyes, the color of newly unearthed amber, seem like two ancient caves. *An archeologist of eyes*; I make a mental note to copy the phrase down in my journal. If only such a profession existed. At the surface, the explorer would see her own reflection, but a good archeologist always digs past the superficial layer – reflecting layer, in the case of the archeologist of eyes. Down into a cavern of experiences, she'd pass shelves, each one housing a year's worth of her subject's memory.

The aquarium in Philadelphia would sit front and center in Grace's six-year shelf: Missy, almost fourteen, taking a turn at the hole-in-one – get all five balls in the middle cup and win a stuffed sea creature.

"Which one?" Missy, bending to eye level, asks a six-year-old Grace.

"The dolphin," she chirps, bouncing with excitement.

Back up one flight to the latest level, the soon-to-be-full seven-year shelf: it's the day after New Years. Still wearing her red negligee, Mom throws on a coat and, shuffling us into her car, heads for the mall. Grace follows Missy and me into the candy store, making a b-line for the rainbow M&M dispenser.

"I got mostly purple and blue." She smiles as we

pay up and walk out. "The blue ones are for Mom."

A crowd has gathered outside the shop, near the second floor escalator. Her shoes and coat in a pile on the floor, Mom paces, muttering to herself and digging her brightly painted nails into her arm. The cluster of curious faces, that security guard who laughed as his partner held Mom's arms behind her back, the bald man who stepped forward, "I'm a doctor. She needs an ambulance right away! Does anyone know this woman?" and Missy covering Grace's mouth before she can scream out – staring at my tiny reflection in Grace's eyes, I'm startled by the sudden appearance of words projected in white on a glossy black screen. *Starring Sheila Davenport, with Sabrina Gibbons, Marissa Gibbons and Grace Davenport*, they read, falling slowly until the last name has disappeared.

"I'll teach you to read!" I blurt out, grabbing Grace's shoulders.

"Hey!" Grace starts, shaking loose.

"What the hell, Bri?" Missy taps my arm. At five-foot seven, she stands just a hairline above me. Our eyes lock and I wince, her stare reminding me of the feral tabby Grace found living under our porch just a few months earlier. *Marissa will survive,* the New York City wind seems to whisper. *She's a tiger among housecats.*

"Grace," Grandma looks up from the note she's been studying. "We're getting you a reading tutor." Taking Grace's hand, she starts toward the cross street. Missy and I bring up the rear. "If worse comes to worse, you'll have to repeat second grade next year."

"That's depends," I counter. "Mom—"

"Mom's not coming." Grandma stops, turning to face Missy and me.

"What?" I feel my chest collapse into my stomach. "How do you know?"

"She called this afternoon."

"Well, where is she?" Reaching out, I grab Missy's arm. It's stiff and I wonder, for a second, if I've accidentally grabbed something else – something stationary and unfeeling. I nudge her, thinking perhaps she missed Grandma's announcement, but she stares off, trance-like.

"Is Mom close?" Grace squirms, yanking Grandma's coat sleeve. "Is she coming for my birthday?"

"I wanted to wait till we got home." Grandma sighs, closing her eyes as she speaks. "Mom's back in Pennsylvania. She isn't coming."

"At all?"

"No, Sabrina. She feels it's best if you girls stay with Grandpa and me from now on."

Hands on my thighs, I bend forward, my legs wobbling beneath my grasp. A light gust shoots by, rustling my hair as it passes. I look up, following the air as it whisks past Grandma, brushing aside a few strands of her brittle, black hair. Wrapped in her fake leopard fur coat, Mom hovers a few feet away, her figure waving gently in the breeze. Smiling, she winks at me. I open my mouth. *Wait! Don't leave!* I'm ready to call out. She extends an arm, holding up one finger. Her round eyes fixed on mine. She takes the orange pill bottle from her coat pocket and, unscrewing the cap, nods. *Szeretlek,* I hear her whisper like a ventriloquist through closed lips. *Don't forget, Bear.* Before I can answer back, repeat the one phrase I know in my grandparents' native tongue, the bottle falls from between her long fingers, spilling a mixture of pebbles and sand.

We walk in silence, Grace dragging her feet as though each stride requires more energy than she can manage. With my coat hood up, I give way to the emotions I wish, like Missy, I could shove into some deep crevice in the lower half of my body. *We'll see her soon,* I reassure myself. *She'll come*, but as hard as I try, I can't let go of the image of Mom's figure fading into the cold January air.

Chapter Five

There's a place I visit when I need to get away; past the roar of Broadway that, even at mid-afternoon, refuses to abate, beyond a row of decrepit brownstones – two of which I swear each time I pass will have crumbled to the pavement by my next trip – to an open, two-way road on 108th Street and Riverside Drive. I close my eyes, breathing in the late January wind as it swishes by, threatening to knock me off the curbside.

The park has three levels. A thin strip, half grass, half pavement, stands above a wider, more rugged field. Past the stone steps and down a steep hill, walking on the balls of my feet to keep my speed in check, I smile at a middle-aged man prying a tennis ball from his yellow lab's mouth Below the middle plain, at the bottom level of Riverside Park, my journey ends. Snug between a baseball field and a skateboard ring, I look out past the Westside Highway at the glistening Hudson River. In my fantasy, the water is freshly salted, as though, perhaps as in a bakery, someone has risen at dawn to scatter handfuls of sea salt from one end to the other. Wearing Mom's old black one-piece, I wade through, the tips of my chestnut hair dragging behind as waves hit my shoulder blades. It isn't long before I make the halfway mark, a sandbar that, in my daydream, rises like a tollbooth to alert the swimmer she is closing in on New Jersey. Here I stop and, standing still against the rushing water, look back at where I started. The rocks, model-size versions of the moors in *Jane Eyre*, lay colorless beneath trees and apartment building tops. To my right, the George Washington Bridge looms, a heavy fog blanketed over each end, making it seem as though cars are headed toward giant cloud puffs that will swallow them whole then spit them out to their final destination. Crouching into shallow diver's position, I prepare to carry onward, this time making the full swim to the other side of The Hudson. *Ready, set,* I begin—

"Go!"

Turning to the familiar voice, I stop. Standing at the edge of a rock, Dad motions toward the water. "Sabrina, go! You can do it."

"Nah-ah. Too deep." From behind my father's thick runner's legs, a little girl emerges. I smile, recognizing her Little Mermaid swimsuit. "Not today."

"Not today?" Dad laughs. "You said that yesterday."

"It's too deep."

"It won't be any less deep tomorrow, Bri."

"I wanna go back to Mom and Missy. It's just too deep today."

"Well," Dad shakes his head, "each day it's gonna seem scarier and scarier. You just gotta *go* for it."

"Maybe tomorrow."

I watch the two figures walk off. My younger self's hand reaches up to grab hold of my father's. They disappear.

~~~~

Missy meets me at the front of our school. "Well," she probes. "How'd you do?"

"Fifty-three." I shrug, taking the exam from my knapsack. "Better than the last one. You know, if we were identical twins, you could take my math tests and I'd write your English essays."

Missy looks up, holding the test in front of her. "This doesn't look that hard. Did you even try?"

"I'm bad at math, Marissa. Damn!" I snatch the exam back, shoving it into the bottom of my bag. "You can be a real jerk, you know that?"

"I'm just saying it doesn't seem super complicated. If you could do Algebra I,—"

"But I didn't do Algebra I, remember?"

"Hey," a blonde girl calls out, walking over to Missy and me. Missy smiles, looking down as the girl flips her pin-straight hair over one shoulder. "Is this your sister?"

"Yeah." Missy fidgets with the sleeve on her new jacket. "This is Bri. Bri, this is Allie."

"Hi," I nod.

"Rissa," Allie begins, stopping to examine my four-year-old coat and washed-out jeans. She raises an eyebrow before turning her back to me. "We're going for pizza. Wanna come?" Allie points to a group of three girls and one boy waiting by the curb.

"Yeah." Missy's eyes widen, her cheeks turning a blush pink. "Just give me one sec."

"Okay." Allie saunters over to the others.

"Rissa?" I snicker.

"Missy just seems childish."

"Well, Rissa, tell Blondie this is the only free period we both have. You can get pizza with her posse another time."

Missy stares at the pavement then turns to the group. "Just this once, Bri? Come on."

My chest tightens and I notice, for the first time, the fraying at the bottom of my coat. I should have made a stink about wearing old clothes to our new school. Perhaps then, like Missy, I'd be accepting invitations to pizza. "Do what you want." I swerve, heading back toward the artificial candy-blue doors.

"Bri, don't be mad, okay?"

I nudge the entrance door open with my foot. *How many smurfs had to die to get this ugly color, anyway?*

"I'll see you later," Missy's call out. I pretend not to hear.

My clothes are old – worn out – my hair ratty. With the exception of a new pair of tennis shoes, I'm the same Sabrina I was before leaving Butler. Sabrina, sometimes Bri – not Rina or Brina. There are no ninety dollar jeans and shiny black ski jackets to hide the fact that I am, for now and always, the daughter of a dead file clerk and an out-of-work actress.

"She'd be really hot if she didn't dress like some homeless grunge kid." The boy's words from my first day sizzle in my ears as I wait for the first floor elevator. Scott Shapiro: by now I know the voice well. He sits behind me during homeroom, sometimes rating the girls in our grade. "Kayla's a perfect ten, should be in porn. Will Chelsea ever get that nose job?" or, this particular morning, telling a story about sleeping with a model at his dad's magazine party.

The numbers above the elevator doors flicker, consecutively turning neon orange – 6, 5, 4 – as though playing a game of hot potato with the burning color. I should take the opportunity to go to Mr Shaffer's homeroom. If he's there, I can ask for an extra tutoring session sometime this week. He'll see that I'm trying; I don't want to fail every Algebra II test this year and have to retake the class over the summer. But then, once Mom comes for us, I won't have to worry about exams at all. We'll move to a small apartment, some place not too expensive. Mom will get a role in an off-Broadway play, maybe not right away, but eventually, and finally be discovered. Missy can stay here if she wants, but I sure as hell won't. In two months I'll be seventeen and, without Grandma and Grandpa telling me what to do, I can drop out and get a job, any job. I'll be able to help Mom with the rent. Working in a bookstore – that would be nice, but honestly, anything's better than this place.

Standing back as the elevator reaches my floor, I settle on going to Mr Shaffer's classroom. Best to work hard for the time being, especially since Mom still hasn't called – not even when Grace turned eight.

"No. Your accent's all wrong." In a faded red dress that hangs down to her ankles, the girl leans against the elevator wall, a grey wig in her left hand. "It's ever-thang. I'm telling you; that's how they say it down there. Ever-thang's up ta date 'n Kansas City." She belts out the last part, smiling as I walk past.

"Ever-tha... no. That's too kitchy." Holding a cowboy hat in front of him, the boy shakes his head.

"It's musical theater. It's supposed to be kitchy. Where's the rest of your outfit?"

"Think my mom put it in with the wash this morning."

Both chuckle as the elevator settles on the basement floor.

"Cameron's going to kill you." The girl laughs. "Will Parker – you're just as dumb as your character."

"Dumb, but irresistible!"

With a rusty hum, the doors open, letting in a surge of voices and piano music. "Bye." The girl turns, nodding toward me. I open my mouth to respond but am silenced as the doors close, shutting out vibrant waves of sound.

Tapping my foot, I peer through the window of Mr Shaffer's homeroom door. Unaware of my presence, he guzzles a can of Pepsi while working through a thick stack of papers. I try not to laugh when, waving his red sharpie as though it was a baton, my math teacher grunts with each stroke of his pen. *At least I don't spend my free time drawing red Xs and making animal noises.* I reach out to turn the handle then stop. *He'd never know if—* I touch the metal lever again. *If I go back downstairs, he'd never know I was here.*

I run through the possible interaction – "Excuse me, Mr Shaffer, could I please speak with you? I'm really struggling in your class."

He'd grunt. "Did you come to the tutoring session I offered before the last test?"

"Yes," I'd say, "but I still failed."

"Then you'll need to hire someone for extra help."

It seems obvious he'll suggest I get someone like the woman who sits at the kitchen table with Grace three times a week. "Now, dear," I'll hear her say from the other end of the apartment. "Let's sound it out together: kit-ten. Kit-ten. Kitten. Very good." I'd rather fail! Right?

Once more I reach for the handle. *"It's musical theater. It's supposed to be kitchy."* Thinking back to the conversation in the elevator, I pause. Which musical? *Singing in the Rain?* No, the girl said something about Kansas City. *The Wizard of Oz?* That starts out in Kansas, right? But it's not really a musical. I peer through the window one last time before turning back toward the elevator. I just need to know which musical. After that, I can worry about Algebra. *Something, something Kansas City.* Mom would know. She wouldn't have to give it a second thought.

The doors open and I stand, for a moment, over the small crack that separates the elevator from the basement floor. A girl's voice carries from behind two closed doors, a sign reading *Oklahoma! rehearsal in progress* taped to the wall. *You just gotta go for it,* I hear my dad say. I step past the gap and toward the theater.

Chapter Six

Nobody seems to notice as I slip through, plopping myself down in the back row. On stage, a girl in a blue and white polka dotted dress clears her throat, her hands firmly on her hips. "You said it was too low last time. Now I'm singing as high as I can, and you're telling me it's still wrong!"

"You need to make it softer," a male voice responds from the front row. I lean forward to see if I can get a better view. "Laurey doesn't belt. She's sweet. Think Julie Andrews, not Ethel Merman."

"Cameron, you're impossible! Why don't you do it, then?"

Laughter ensues. "Yeah!" Another boy in the front row points his cowboy hat at the stage. I recognize his voice as the one I heard earlier in the elevator. "Come on, Cameron. I wanna hear your sweet Julie Andrews voice."

"Shut it, Aaron. I'll listen to your ideas when you can remember to bring your costume." The boy, Cameron, hops on stage. "Guys, we go on next week!

Aaron, you can't be Will Parker without the cowboy boots, dirty jeans and all. What happens if you forget your costume next Wednesday, huh?" Cameron turns to the girl on stage. "You keep forgetting who Laurey is. She's tough, yeah; like she says in her song, she won't go crying over some random guy, but she's also pure and soft. When Jud tries to take advantage—" Eyeing me, Cameron pauses. I sink into my seat, the cushion's rough material itching my exposed skin. "Hey," he calls out. "Are you part of the production? I don't—" He jumps down from the stage, walking toward me. "You're not supposed to be here if you're not part of the show."

Shit! I spring to my feet, my mind racing. *I thought this was... what? What do I say? What's my excuse?* Everyone turns, staring as though I were the actor on stage.

Standing just a few feet away, Cameron squints, crossing his arms. "I know you."

"No." I back up, reaching for the door. "I made a mistake. I thought my English class was in here today."

"No, I remember." He points, wagging his finger at me. "I saw you outside the school. I remember because I'd never seen you before then. You were with an older woman and a little girl."

I clench my fists, running through the past few weeks as fast as I can. It has been almost a month since we started at Whitman Prep. Grandma picked us up a few times, maybe three or four, until Missy and I got the hang of getting around on our own. Now when Grandma gets Grace, I'm usually gone – sitting in Riverside Park, reading or writing in my journal. Perhaps we passed each other during that first week, but

I can't remember. I turn to leave, when Cameron calls out, "Hey. Your stuff."

I swivel back around, eager to get outside. With History class in five minutes, I'll only have a few moments to stand by the entrance doors and breathe in the refreshing winter air.

"Your bag."

Taking my knapsack, I look up at Cameron, a run-of-the-mill thank-you smile forming on my lips. Then I remember – *curious eyes. You were the one with curious eyes,* I want to say, staring at the aquamarine disks surrounding his two piercing pupils. "I do remember." The words spill out, unexpected. "My first day; I saw... you were leaving school. That was my first day." I look down, embarrassed by my sloppy response.

"Was that your little sister?"

"Grace." I nod. "She hated her first day." The image of Grace sobbing into my coat whisks through my memory like a swift breeze.

"Well," Cameron turns, looking back at the stage. "We don't usually let people watch pre-production. It takes away from the final experience, you know. If you see a show during the rehearsal phase—"

"It's like seeing a baby before it's been born. My mother... I've heard that before." My cheeks sting. I imagine every ounce of blood in my body springing to my face, and forming the reddest, dopiest blush ever. The front of the theater is silent.

"You—" Cameron cocks his head, studying me as though I were a difficult equation, or some strange painting he can't quite interpret. "You know a lot about theater?"

"No." My fingers grasp for the door handle. I shake my head. "I don't know anything."

"Hey."

I turn once more, half my body out of the theater.

"You can come back if you want. Just don't tell your friends or anything."

Right. Which friends? I smile. "Thanks."

~~~~

Mom's old bed squeaks as I roll, changing positions with every passing thought. *1:15 AM,* the alarm clock reads. *Damn!* Sitting up, I flip on the nightlight. My journal lies face down, a pen lodged between the pages holding my latest entry. I have math first thing in the morning. With no sleep, I'll be totally useless when Mr Schaffer discusses, as he said he would last class, imaginary numbers. What the hell is an imaginary number, anyway? If something's imaginary, why study it? How can you study it? Venturing down the hall, journal in hand, I shuffle toward the kitchen. Missy's light is still on, but I'm not surprised. She's never been one for sleep.

Parting the knob-less wooden doors, more like swinging white slabs, really, I'm startled as Grandma looks up, two cardboard shoeboxes placed on the table in front of her. "Can't sleep?" Her worn eyes – slightly puffy and red – greet mine. I wonder if she's been crying.

"No. Too much on my mind."

"Me, too. Come," Grandma gestures, pulling out a chair.

The overhead lamp gleams, illuminating each item

on the wooden table, and I am reminded of my afternoon encounter in the theater. I lay my journal on the kitchen stage.

"Is that for school?" Grandma nods.

"No. It's personal." I flip the diary over, underlining the front quote with my finger. "Mom got it for me for Christmas."

Smiling, Grandma reaches out and brushes my cheek. "I kept one of those when I was your age, back in Hungary. Come to think of it, I don't remember if it had any words on the cover. No, it was plain – just plain and brown. I wrote all my secrets in that book." Getting up, Grandma winks. "I need some tea; something good and strong. Sleep isn't in the cards for tonight."

"Can I have some too?" I peer over, trying to get a look at what's in the two boxes.

"Yes, of course. Don't be shy. There's nothing top secret in those."

I reach for the box nearest me. Beneath the bent lid are two stacks of photos. The first is a faded black-and-white of a small cottage, *Eger, 1953,* written in black ink on the back.

"Is that you?" I ask, turning to the next: a girl, tall and slender, her hair coiled in a perfect dancer's bun, posing at a ballet bar.

Shuffling over, an unopened box of Earl Grey in one hand, Grandma takes the picture, grinning as she holds it up to the light. "I would have been about your age. Maybe a little older."

"Mom told me you were a ballerina."

"Oh?" Grandma lays the photo on the table, moving back to the stove. "What else did she tell you?"

"Just that you danced before the war. Before you and Grandpa—"

With one sharp turn of the knob, a steady flame, blue and orange, springs from beneath the kettle. I pause, wondering, as I always do, if it's true that blue fire is the hottest of all. "Before you ran away."

"Ran away?" Returning to her seat, Grandma pushes the shoebox aside. "We... it wasn't running away. Cowards run, Sabrina. Kalman and I were not cowards."

"But you left Hungary because of a war, right?"

"You know about World War II, no?"

I nod. "Of course."

"Grandpa and I were children then. Our country had already seen great suffering at the end of the first world war. I was only four when the second began, ten when it ended. Grandpa was thirteen. I remember little of that time, but, to be Hungarian, it was no easy matter. My parents kept our culture alive at home, but outside, to keep trouble away, we played a part – especially in that last year when the Germans occupied. We were all actors then, saluting the SS Troops when they rode through, studying German in school like it was superior to what our ancestors spoke. You see, we had enemies all around. We needed protection, from the Soviets most of all, but when the Germans were defeated, the Soviets moved in. Sabrina," Grandma places her hand on my arm. "Like your mother, I was the youngest – the only daughter. My father and brothers worked hard to spare me from the horrors around us, but I heard about the executions, the labor camps, at school, took notice when a classmate didn't show up. A week would pass and we'd learn her father was a democrat, taken from the home by Soviet troops. Those who were taken never returned.

"Yes, like other girls, I rode my bike, dreamed of romance and becoming a famous ballerina – the Hungarian Anna Pavlova." Leaning back, Grandma fixes her stare on the overhead light. "I would show them all that way. A dark girl from the Hungarian countryside could do it just as well... no, better than any Russian. I would dance the greatest dying swan the world had ever seen." Grandma reaches over, placing the lid back on the box of photographic memories. "Well, in nineteen fifty-four my life really did change." With a startling hum, the teakettle lurches. Like a train readying for departure, it settles, lurches once more, then sputters, letting out clouds of steam through its tube-shaped snout. Placing two mugs on the table, Grandma pours scalding water. I watch the clear liquid muddy as it hits my tea bag.

"My middle brother, Stephen, your uncle's namesake, brought a young man to our home – Kalman Farkas, the son of a well respected mathematician from Budapest. He spoke of resistance, secretly read Karl Marx and knew that real communism was not what the Soviets represented. Freedom for Hungary, he said, was worth dying for. My father went to great lengths to get this young, city rebel out of our home, but as they say, the seeds of dissent had been planted. For my brothers, that is and for me; I would have gone anywhere for this man."

As I lean my restless head against the palm of my hand, I think about love – sensual love that, as I have read in books and seen in movies, has the power to possess a person completely, unrelentingly, like an intoxicating phantom. Jane Eyre resorts to running away and begging in the streets when she learns of Mr Rochester's wife. At the end of *Camille,* Marguerite rejoices in the arms of her lover as she dies, having sacrificed everything for Armand. The image of Greta Garbo's face greeting death with a smile drifts by, waving as it glides through my memory. Then, with a shudder, I turn my thoughts to real life. I see Dad driving through a mid-winter snowstorm, clutching a picture of Mom (it was later found pressed against the dashboard). So why do we do it, then – dream of falling into this trance that drives us straight into the deep end? It seems so stupid, like those animals Missy told me about that gather together just to dive off a cliff. Well, I refuse!

Looking up at the dusky overhead light, I remember Cameron's commanding voice. He was like a police officer charging toward me, ready to send me running from the theater, when something changed. As he looked at me, really saw me up close, he softened.

Grandma continues, smoothing my hair behind my ear. "When you love someone like I've loved your grandfather, and he's loved me, you grow a second heart. As silly to you as that may sound, it is true. I had one heart that beat steadily for my family, my parents and brothers, but then another grew when I met Kalman, and its rhythm was for him and our country, our future. You see, there is no future in a state of oppression. I figured that, so in nineteen fifty-five, tossing my ballet aside, I went with Kal to Budapest. My brothers followed. We were prepared for death, no matter how terrible. We would help build an army that could rid Hungary once and for all of the leeches, the

Soviets, Nazis, and whatever new group might come along to soil our great nation with regulations that were not of our choosing. The future would be ours – a future of freedom."

"So you and Grandpa fought then?" I ask, imagining Mom must have been mistaken. They ran away during the war, she'd said.

"It was our plan..." Pausing, Grandma spreads her hand out, palm down, on the table. Take away the wrinkles, and it would be almost identical to my mother's. "...Until the summer of nineteen fifty-six when I found out I was pregnant. The Resistance grew strong, about three thousand Hungarians ready to die in the name of freedom – my brothers Stephen and Tibor were among them. Kal would have been, too, until he learned we were to have a child. We'd been married in a small church just after we arrived in Budapest. As a wife and partner in the revolution, my life was in great danger. I'd been prepared for that, prepared to die for my country. All of that changed when I learned I was going to be a mother. Kal and I made it back to my parents' home on August twentieth, Saint Stephen's Day, a good omen we thought. We weren't there on the front lines when the revolution broke out. My brother Stephen was the first to die, then Tibor. Neither had the satisfaction of seeing the Soviets retreat, running like cowards from the city as October came to an end. When the borders opened in early November, Kal and I left. My father arranged it, risked everything to get us out. We traveled to England, where your uncle Stephen was born. Then we came to the U.S. Kal set up his business here in New York and we counted our blessings. Yes, our country was in shambles. We knew and suffered on the inside, but I made a promise to God, and so did your grandfather. We raised Stephen, Victor and Sheila in a Hungarian home. We taught them to love their heritage and culture. You know, your mother's first word was *apa*, father in Hungarian. She barely spoke a word of English until she was four. So, when she says to you, 'Grandma and Grandpa ran away from the war,' you must know that we did not run as cowards. We sought asylum as parents because there was no other choice."

"I—" Getting up, I carry my untouched cup of tea to the sink. *3:00 AM*, the clock on the microwave reads. I roll my eyes at the thought of an 8:40 math class. "I'm glad you didn't stay. In Hungary, I mean."

"Oh?" Grandma's eyes widen as she lifts her chin. I wish I could have met her at sixteen. *Would we have been friends?* I wonder.

"Because then you and grandpa might have been killed. I wouldn't be here. Neither would Missy and Grace."

"Yes." A calm seems to wash over Grandma's countenance. As her face relaxes, I feel a bubble of warmth float my way. My eyes grow heavy as it travels through my limbs. I know I will be able to sleep now.

"Mom did teach me one phrase in Hungarian." I push open the heavy swinging doors.

"What?"

"Szeretlek."

"Very good," Grandma grins. "Nagyon Szeretlek."

"What's that?"

"I love you very much."

Chapter Seven

It's an unusual February day. Though the trees are bare, pierced by yesterday's winter chill, the steady sun breathes yellow warmth, allowing for a break in the pattern, an early taste of natural regeneration. I round the corner, my coat tied around my waist, carrying the book Grandma surprised me with the night before. "I noticed you carrying *Jane Eyre* around," she smiled. "So funny. This was your mom's; one of her favorites."

The worn copy of *Wuthering Heights* has a painting of a doll-faced girl on the cover. Her heart-shaped lips remind me of my own. This morning I decided to borrow one of Grandma's ribbon-pink lipsticks. Missy, or Rissa, as she now insists on being called, begged me to take it off. "You look like a clown," she scoffed.

It doesn't matter. I am headed to school, a book written by my favorite author's younger sister under my arm. I am sure Emily never told Charlotte she looked like a clown. The rest just seems trivial.

Relaxed on the second step, I can't help but admire the turquoise front doors, how they inspire, especially under a generous sun, the white stone building to glow. Other schools from our past visits to New York had what Whitman Prep offers: impossible (for me) math classes, snooty girls, jerky guys and everything else that always made Missy and me relieved when, after about a month or two, Mom would announce, "We're going home. Pack your things." It felt good, for a short while, to do the things normal girls do, but there was always a strand, like an invisible leash, yanking us back to our life in Pennsylvania where real school was never a possibility.

With Jim gone much of the time, his truck parked outside some sleazy bar, I'd bet, in Missouri or Arkansas or wherever his job took him, we'd have a few hours here and there to look over the booklets we received from the Christian Life Homeschooling Society while Mom went out or kept busy. We never made it to any of the gatherings, though, or got to meet other homeschooled students because "It's mostly nonsense," Mom would say. "Don't believe any of the God stuff. These books are the cheapest. Just learn what makes sense, enough to pass those damn state tests. What really matters in life – I can teach you that."

She did: how to recite lines with aching passion, ways to summon emotion – cry on command – and the histories of her favorite actors. "Acting is the most personal, honest profession in the world," she'd say. "Just look." Pointing to John Gilbert's face when he sees, for the first time, Greta Garbo in *Queen Christina*, Mom would hit the pause button. "Grace, pumpkin, what do you see on that man's face?"

"He looks sad."

"Exactly! Do you know why?"

Grace would shake her head, Daisy Girl pressed against her chest.

"This was the first film Gilbert and Garbo made after she left him standing at the altar – a no-show at her own wedding! You see? Look how magnificent they are right here in this scene. All that raw emotion: that comes from real life!"

Sometimes Missy and I would take the bus to the public library. There she'd talk to Chris, the engineering student who volunteered on his days off. While they spoke numbers and equations, I'd sift through the novels, looking for something to whisk me off into another time, another family. I ached for a father like Atticus in *To Kill a Mockingbird*, a sister like Beth in *Little Women,* but it was *Jane Eyre* that drew me in over and over, taking my hand and, with a gentle tug, leading me through the open archway that divides our world from the many worlds of fiction. Perhaps it was her adventures, each one, no matter how heartbreaking, turning out all right in the end. Or was it her resilience, her ability, though parentless and, at times, with nothing but hope to carry her forward, to build a life of her own, a family of her choosing because her real family could never really come through? Each time I opened Charlotte Brontë's novel I felt, in the center of my rib cage, a ripple of hope for myself, hope for what might one day be a life of my own, a life of my choosing.

Taking one last look at the girl on the cover's pale, vacant stare, I am reminded of Grace. Grace will be pretty, perhaps the prettiest of all three of us, but always empty, borrowing bits and pieces from those around her because there's never enough... never enough inner substance to fill her up. I open to the first page and step through.

"What's that?"

Half way to the bottom of page one I look up. As though he can't manage to wait for my response, Cameron squats, the top of his head level with my chin, and peers under my knees. I resist the urge to scratch the back of his neck as he looks with his head strained awkwardly, like a parrot begging for attention.

"*Wuthering Heights*."

"I see." Cameron fingers his chin, the small stalks of blonde stubble sparkling under the bright sun. He squints, grinning like a satisfied housecat. "Blowing off class to read, Miss Gibbons." He recites my name drawing out each syllable.

"Nope. I have a free period Tuesday mornings, Mr.—" *Theater Nazi?*

"Bodie. Cameron Bodie."

"Got it," I nod. "How'd you learn my last name?"

"Asked around. It wasn't as easy as I'd have thought, though. Apparently you keep to yourself." Cameron shifts to sit by my side.

I shrug. "The people here aren't exactly friendly. I don't have much of a choice."

"Which homeroom are you in again?"

"Eleven D."

"Well that explains it. I'd hide out if I had to see Scott Shapiro every day too."

"And Chelsea and Kayla," I add, sticking *Wuthering Heights* in my knapsack.

"Christ! They must have hated you to put you in

with those people."

"Probably." It feels good to laugh along. I like the way the ridge on Cameron's nose wrinkles when he smiles. Would Mom find him handsome? I can't quite tell.

"Are they still together?"

"Who?"

"Scott and Kayla. I don't know. They've been on and off since freshman year. I had homeroom with them last year – lots of drama, but not the good kind."

"I haven't a clue." Resting on my elbows, I close my eyes and let the sun warm my cheeks. A group of students pass by. I'm sure at least one has given me a dirty look, but it doesn't matter. This evening, my half Eastern European skin will be a shade darker. Missy will harass me about my clothes, my clownish lipstick, but I'll be the one with the glowing tan – a tan she could never get without reddening like a ready-to-be-picked radish.

"Well, I kinda expected to see you last week. Could've used some help, you know."

"I was busy." Sitting up, I glare at Cameron. The memory of him storming toward me in the theater makes me scowl. "Plus, you made it pretty clear I wasn't wanted."

Cameron's face drops. He looks down, flicking a crumpled leaf off the step. "Yeah, I'm sorry about that. It's just... well, for one thing, we really don't like people who aren't part of the production watching rehearsals."

"I wasn't hurting anyone."

"I know." Cameron looks up. "But also, I guess I thought you were one of those – like Scott, or Kayla or

Chelsea... just at first. I thought you were there to mock us."

As our eyes lock, a flicker of hurt washes over Cameron. He winces as if to free himself from it, squeeze it out the way you would a piece of debris that has lodged beneath your eyelid, but it's still there, visible and painful, all the same.

"My mother's an actress, a great one." The words flow freely, without much need for forethought. "She taught us to love the theater. Acting is sacred, the most honest job on the planet. The best times of my life were when she was rehearsing for a play. She was happy then. Dad, Missy – my sister – and I counted the days, marked the kitchen calendar because we could hardly wait to see her opening night. I'd never mock anyone in a theater. Never."

Cameron reaches out, brushes my arm for a split second, then recoils. "A bug." He jolts as though zapped by a shockwave. "Sorry. I thought there was a bug on your arm."

I turn to the school doors, smiling at the deep, shining blue. I half expect them to smile back.

"Do you wanna come to *Oklahoma!* tomorrow? It's our first performance, starts at seven. If you're free maybe you could come by after school. We're doing a quick run-through before, getting out the kinks and stuff. It may be boring but I'd like to know what you think. It's my first time directing – you could say my directorial debut. That's what I want to do... with my life I mean. I want to be a director. I guess this is my first shot."

"Okay." Trying not to look too enthusiastic, I offer a half-smile; not an easy performance when I could squeal with excitement. "Tomorrow after school? I think I could do that."

"Thanks, Sabrina. By the way, did you ever see that movie?"

"Which movie?" In less than ten minutes I'll be expected to complete an endurance test in the gymnasium. My thoughts shift to possible excuses. *I can't exercise today because…*

"The one with… oh, what's her name?"

I've twisted my what? Broken my…

"Audrey Hepburn. The movie *Sabrina* with Audrey Hepburn."

Mother. Broken my mother. "What?" I feel a surge leap up my stomach, constricting my chest and throat before it tumbles out through my mouth and into the open moment. "My mother." The surge glides off. I brace to reach out, grab hold before it evaporates, but I'm still as it melds with the rest of the warm air. "Sorry. What?" I cough.

"I just asked if you saw the movie *Sabrina.*" Cameron raises his eyebrows quizzically.

"Yes. I was named… my mother named me after that movie." An image of Mom back in Pennsylvania dangles in the front of my mind. Is she working? Saving up to move here? Has she gotten rid of Jim, this time for good? I could try calling the house for the hundredth time, but it would be no use. The number hasn't been in service for a while now.

"That's pretty awesome. To be named after a movie, I mean. You must love your name. Cameron's Scottish. It means crooked nose or something lame like that." Cameron scrunches his face. "I don't think it really fits me. Do you?" With his index finger he tilts his nose to one side.

"Hmm, maybe a little," I chuckle. "But only a little."

"Well, I'll allow you that one insult, Miss Gibbons, but I expect your undivided attention tomorrow. My nose and I can be forgiving to a helpful director's assistant."

"Well," I rise to head off to gym class. "I hope I am helpful."

"I'm sure you will be. And Sabrina—"

I turn back. "Yeah?"

"Don't let the Scotts and Kaylas make you wanna hide out. They don't run the school, you know."

"Okay." I enter the building, noticing a gentle swish as a puff of wind sneaks in behind me. It settles on the back of my neck, homeless now that it has been shut in.

Chapter Eight

Sporting a black jacket and khaki pants, Cameron stands by the gaping theater doors, handing out playbills printed on paper from the school library. He winks at me as I take one of the hand-folded booklets. "You're up front with me," he whispers. "First row, center. My seat's the one with sneakers under it." I look down at his black shiny loafers. "Yeah," his voice follows as I'm ushered into the dimly lit room. "Men's dress shoes are uncomfortable too, you know." He is adorable, I admit, taking my seat next to the one with two worn running shoes hidden from plain view. It's too bad I've sworn never to fall in love.

I feel like an insider looking at the bare stage, holding some idea of what's happening behind the black platform. Parents, students and teachers shuffle in, beaming over the prospect of seeing their kid, friend or star pupil perform. I imagine Aaron's parents clutching their playbills, having just pointed to their son's name at the top of the cast list, while Aaron is backstage working hard to perfect that drawl I explained would be crucial to a southern character. "You see!" Cameron exclaimed as Aaron looked sheepishly at the floor. "It's not kitschy; it's accurate. Sabrina, can you show him?"

"I can't sing."

"Doesn't matter. Just do the accent."

With a deep breath, I did. "Ever-thang's up ta date 'n Kaynsus City."

"So I really have to draw out all my words?" Aaron's freckled skin reddened.

"Yes."

"What makes you the expert?" Skylar, the girl playing Laurey, asked, her arms crossed.

She and Aaron have been a couple for two years, Cameron explained during a break. She's known for getting quite defensive... possessive, too. "A bit of a loose cannon," Cameron had whispered, "but one hell of an actress."

"For one thing, I lived in the south for some time. I know the accent. Also—" I paused, deciding not to bring up my mother – how she spent hours teaching us different accents. "I just lived in the south, so I know."

Leaning back in my seat, I consider the story of *Oklahoma!* Laurey, a farm girl who lives with her aunt, is in love with Curly, a cowboy, but she's also tough and not so sure about giving all her love to one man. Curly loves Laurey too but, as a cowboy, he has to be careful because cowboys don't marry farm girls. Laurey's best friend, Annie, is also a farm girl with a super protective father. Though she loves a guy named Will Parker, she can't help flirting with other men when Will's not around. Like Curly, Will's also a cowboy.

Anyway, there's a creepy guy named Jud who works on Laurey's aunt's farm. He's obsessed with Laurey and tries to take advantage of her. When Laurey rejects Jud, he threatens her. Curly promises to protect Laurey, and they get married. Jud attacks Curly, but Curly kills Jud. In the end, all is well and good. Curly gets Laurey, and Will gets Annie.

Though I know the music is famous and all, I'm not sure I care too much for the storyline. Real life just isn't like that. Not everyone who deserves it gets a happy ending. It doesn't happen.

"Are you ready?" Cameron asks, taking his seat. "Here we go." He reaches across the armrest, inching toward my hand, then pulls back, shifting his gaze to the soon-to-be bustling stage. Looking down, I notice my hand is open, cupped as though ready to receive or give an offering. I squeeze it shut and wince, my nails scratching my naked palm.

~ ~ ~ ~

Strolling past the rows of apartment buildings on West End Avenue, I can't get the tune of *People Will Say We're in Love* out of my head. Cameron was right; though her voice wasn't perfect, Skylar acted beautifully. She and Aaron stole the show, no two ways about it. If Mom had been there, she would have been impressed, even if she refused to admit it.

As the curtain fell after the last act, Cameron grasped my hand. "We did it," he smiled.

My legs warm and tingly, I leaned over, not wanting to scream above the rounds of clapping. "You did it." Then it happened, just the way you sometimes blurt out a word without knowing where it came from. I kissed him on the cheek. For the first time since Dad died, I kissed a man on the cheek. As I pulled away, Cameron's face flushed, his eyes wide, clear as newly-surfaced sea glass; I knew I'd stepped into something new, something I'd vowed to never let happen. I was beginning to fall in love.

Still humming, I open the apartment door. Sitting cross-legged in the middle of the hallway, Grace springs to her feet. "I've been waiting here forever!" she says, scuttling toward me. The image of a dog pining for her master takes center stage, shoving remnants from *Oklahoma!* into the foreground. Grace points to Missy's bedroom. It is at this moment that I become aware of my sister's slurred, fury-filled words.

"You're a fucking fascist!" Missy hollers.

"Don't you dare speak to me like that!" Grandma shrieks in return.

Something is thrust across the room, shattering as it reaches a landing.

Taking my hand, Grace leads me into the kitchen. Grandpa sits at the table, his head bowed over the portable telephone.

"What happened?" I try to rewind, float back to where I was just minutes before entering into a chaos I know only too well, but this time it isn't Mom's drunken ramblings, her careless hurling of insults. It isn't Jim throwing ashtrays or lamps and wheeling obscenities.

Grandpa massages his temples. "Marissa came home reeking of alcohol. Horrible. All we did was try to talk to her and you'd have thought she was possessed. I can't do this again, Sabrina. Not again."

Grandpa shakes his head, his thick hands shielding his eyes.

A door slams. "Did you call the police, Kalman?" Her hair out of place, cheeks the color of ripe tomatoes, Grandma huffs, stomping into the kitchen.

Grandpa grabs the phone, holding it in the other direction at arm's length. "No."

"Give it to me now," Grandma barks.

Squeezing me tight around the middle, Grace whimpers, her bony shoulders trembling. "They're gonna take Missy away now, too," she heaves.

"What?" A few octaves lower, but still elevated to a yell, Grandma prods. "What was that?" She taps Grace on the shoulder.

"Don't yell at me!"

Kneeling to Grace's eye level, Grandma places her long fingers on her back. "Come, come. Shh. I didn't mean to yell at you."

Fingers in her mouth, Grace wipes her nose on her pajama sleeve. She plops down on the kitchen floor. I stand silent and still, my back to the kitchen doors.

"Kalman, put the phone back," Grandma orders, but Grandpa doesn't move. He clutches the phone as though it were a treasure – the very last of its kind.

Grace stares up at me. She sniffles, her chin quivering.

"Go on," I nod.

"What did you mean, Grace?" Grandma joins her on the almost spotless white tiled floor.

"The police got Mommy." Sliding her fingers from her lips, Grace leaves a trail of saliva on her chin. She wipes it with the back of her hand. "That time. Remember, Bri?"

I shrug, looking at the kitchen window. Against a navy sky, the pane acts as a projection screen. I see all four of us, small but clear. *Just a typical kitchen scene*, I whisper to myself. *Typical. That is all.* "Uh-huh." I turn to Grace, then Grandma. "It happened less than two months ago."

"The police came for Momma?" Grandma raises her left brow.

"At the mall," I begin. "We—"

Pushing his chair from under him, Grandpa gets up. He walks past me, straight through the heavy swinging doors, not even bothering to use his hand to part them. I picture a soldier walking into the line of fire, broken and defeated.

"She was… it was the day after New Years. She wanted to go for a drive." I cover my eyes with the back of my hand, my face scrunching involuntarily. "I want… I know she's sick or crazy or something, but I wanted to think it would be different. Every year I want that," I retch. "But it never happens! Even if I say those things, those things you say to make it better, it never does! It never does."

Grandma reaches up. "Come. Come to me," she beckons. I sink to the floor, clutching her hand. Grace snuggles next to me, sniffling softly. She's learned, I realize, to quiet herself when others are in pain. It's as though her feelings concede to those of the people around her. She'd been a quiet baby, only crying when no one else was in crisis. With Mom and Jim as parents, that was practically never.

"Momma's very, very sick," Grandma whispers.

"Is she going to die?" Grace starts, grabbing hold of my arm.

"It's not that kind of sick. It isn't a sickness of the body."

Grace settles, still clutching me for support.

"What your Momma has is a sickness of the mind."

The image of Bertha, Mr Rochester's first wife in *Jane Eyre*, flashes before me. I can see her, scurrying around on all fours, howling like an animal. To me, Bertha always seemed proof that Mom wasn't mad. If madness meant something so extreme as barking on the floor like a dog, Mom, to my great relief, didn't fit the standard. I wonder, waiting for Grandma to continue, to give an explanation for why our mother has struggled all these years, if a part of me didn't know, didn't suspect that what Mom described as artistic eccentricity was, in fact, a definable illness.

"It's called Bipolar Disorder." Grandma's voice wavers as she pronounces *disorder*. She clears her throat, regaining full composure. I can imagine her as a girl my age, perhaps a tad older, dancing for hours on end. Any sign of exhaustion or discomfort would be met with self-discipline and resilience. She'd suffer through it. "They used to call it Manic Depression. I don't know why the name changed, but when Momma was a teenager, about Marissa's age, the troubles began."

I hug my knees to my chest. Watching me, Grace does the same. "What happened?" I settle my head against the kitchen table's leg.

"The first episode – that's what they're called; episodes – happened just before the start of a new school year. Tenth grade, it was. Sheila – Momma..." Grandma turns to Grace, smoothing her hair. "...wouldn't get out of bed. She cried in her room, and barely ate. We thought it was just moods – regular girl moods, if you know what I mean. She missed the first week of school, but I called her in sick. 'I'll take her to see the doctor,' I told myself. 'If this doesn't pass soon, I'll take her.' Then one morning she got up, ate a huge breakfast, and I remember because she was such a beautiful girl, she put on tight jeans and a colorful top. Her hair was carefully brushed, not one strand out of place, and curled at the bottom. Beautiful. She was so excited to be back in school, which was unusual because Momma never much liked school. Oh, she was smart as a whip," Grandma assures, "but never one to be told what to do. Well, that morning she, your uncle Victor and Grandpa sat at the table and laughed. I thanked God. 'Bless you for bringing my Sheila back,' I said. She was just wonderful, in such high spirits."

Grandma pauses, closing her eyes. I think back to the idea I conjured, the Archeologist of Eyes. Looking at Grandma now, I cannot read those sharp, bark-colored ovals, memory-makers that have seen wartime suffering and defeat, pain that could harden and dry up even the most resilient. Now they shut the door, lock me out, but I wait patiently, because I know they will open back up to draw me in once more. I will step through, sit still while the story, the tale that tortures my Grandmother most, unfurls before me.

"She talked all the time, almost to no end," Grandma continues, her eyes wide like someone who has woken from a long, dream-filled sleep. "Always making plans. Going to Hollywood, that was what she wanted. I said to her we'll see. We'll see if your grades improve this year. Then we can decide. It was a precious week, but..." Releasing a heavy sigh,

Grandma tilts her head to the floor. "...the change came swiftly, like a bullet through a clear night sky. The constant chatter became, well, almost absurd. She spoke so quickly that it was hard to keep up, to understand, but you couldn't say slow down – not without making her angry.

"One morning Victor came into the kitchen. 'Sheila's lost her marbles,' he said. 'Just listen to her in the bedroom.' I went to sit her down to try to understand this seeking for attention, this strange way of acting. I could hear her speaking, stomping around. I knocked three times: nothing, no response, so I opened the door." Grandma turns to me, then Grace. "She'd taken the scissors from the kitchen and cut off all her hair. It lay in clumps all over the floor. She began to scream when she saw me. 'Make it stop!' She was crying, breathing heavy. Grandpa rushed in, and I called the hospital while he held her. She screamed and cried, thrashing around until the ambulance came. They gave her a shot, something – I can't remember the name – and they took her. Momma was in the hospital for a little over one month that time. They found just the right medication. It's an art they say: picking the right kind and knowing how much to use. Well, that was just the first time. That was the first episode, anyway."

"But she got worse?" I probe. "Even with medicine?"

"She was okay for a while, but you must remember that this was the beginning of the eighties and, in New York City, life was fast – faster than it had ever been. Momma wanted to be like the other kids. She didn't want to just live quietly, taking her medication like she needed to and resting. She didn't want a slow life. She wanted grandeur and excitement. She began to drink and use drugs, staying out at all hours against our wishes. It didn't matter how many rules we set; she'd break them all without a care in the world. For a beautiful, spirited girl like Sheila, those nightclubs were the worst places she could be." Grandma gets up, messaging her back as she straightens. "This is old business, and I'm very tired."

I stand, taking Grace by the arm. Amid the past-midnight quiet, I listen for noises in the hallway. All is hushed. Though her light is still on, Missy must have fallen asleep.

"Can I stay in here tonight?" Grace sniffles, trailing behind me as I come to my... Mom's old room. It's hard, as I turn the knob, to stop the thought of Mom pacing about, slicing off chunks of her thick, teenage hair, from keeping me still, frozen stiff at her old bedroom door. Somehow I half expect her to be in there. Giving way to the image I allow myself, for a moment, to picture what it must have been like. There she is, her back to me, those long fingers clutching a pair of scissors. She turns abruptly, letting out a moan. I gasp. The body is that of my mother: the stunning beige skin, long arms scattered with Marilyn Monroe beauty marks, but it's Missy's face that confronts me, glowering like a savage wildcat.

"Please!" Grace tugs at my shirtsleeve. "Just this one time."

I turn to her, cupping her small face in my hands. "For tonight, okay."

Grace and I fall asleep, her arm around my middle. Daisy Girl rests, snug between our bodies.

Chapter Nine

Notebooks snap shut, perfectly synchronized with the tick of the clock on the front wall. As always I wait, giving Mr Shaffer a chance to confirm with an emphatic nod that yes, class is, in fact, over. I wonder, piling pencil and notepad into my knapsack, if it even makes a difference. In Pennsylvania or Virginia, you'd be burned alive for some of the behavior my classmates get away with. True, I never went to high school in either state, but there's no way a student could just slam her book shut and get up to leave at Roanoke Baptist Elementary without a teacher's permission. Judging from Mr Shaffer's indifferent stare, I get the impression he's so used to typical New York high school rudeness that he doesn't notice my attempt at showing respect. He's going to fail me regardless.

Last one through the door, as always, I quicken my step, eager to meet Cameron at the front entrance. We've planned to go down into Riverside Park and watch cars speed by on the Westside Highway while the boats glide calmly across the Hudson, and talk. Before getting on the elevator, I decide to make a quick stop at the girls' room to fix my hair and put on a touch of lip gloss just to add a little shine – nothing fancy.

"Serena," I hear someone say as I look into the large bathroom mirror. Two girls come and stand at my side.

"Sabrina," I correct Chelsea for perhaps the fiftieth time. At this point I know she does it just to be rude. Either that or she has some serious memory problems.

I turn to face Chelsea and Kayla. Both glare at me, their arms folded, standing in the exact same position. What's the word? Automaton! That's what Cameron calls them – twin automatons.

"What?" I place my hands on my hips. I've got a bipolar mom, a piece of shit stepdad and now a sister who stays out late most nights then comes home drunk, high and throwing tantrums you'd expect from a four-year-old Park Avenue princess – something Kayla and Chelsea might actually know something about. I'm not going to let two spoiled morons intimidate me.

"Is Rissa, that girl in tenth grade, your sister?" Kayla flips her wavy auburn hair over one shoulder.

I shrug. "Yeah. So?"

"Well, you need to tell her to stay in her own grade."

"I have no idea what you're talking about." I drop my lip gloss back into my bag. If Kayla were an animal, she'd be a stealthy jaguar. I can see her slinking behind bushes, still full from an earlier meal, waiting to pounce on some unsuspecting young animal. She'd have no desire to eat it. She'd kill simply for the sake of killing.

"You know Scott? Scott Shapiro?" Kayla continues.

"Kind of. We're in homeroom and a few classes together. We don't talk or anything."

"Well, your sister's been hooking up with him."

Chelsea nods in confirmation.

"It stops now."

I stare straight into Kayla's prowling eyes. "My sister doesn't tell me anything, so I really don't know what you're talking about, but if you think—"

"Your sister's a slut."

"Get out of my way!" I rush toward the door. Grabbing my arm, Kayla stares me down. This time I cower, avoiding her glare.

"Tell your slut sister to stay the fuck away from Scott Shapiro, because if she doesn't, she'll be sorry. Believe me."

Shaking loose, I kick open the door and run to the elevator.

"Sabrina?" I hear Mr Shaffer say as I pass him. I don't stop.

~ ~ ~ ~

"Hey, what's wrong?" Cameron places his hand on my quivering shoulder.

"Nothing. Can we just go now?"

"You look like you're either going to cry or beat someone to death. Can I at least know which it is? I do value my life, you know."

I feel a grin, big and dopey, stretch across my face. *Damn! He can always make me smile.*

Cameron's sturdy hand in mine – "the Bodie's are Scottish," he's explained. "We're a stocky bunch" – we stroll toward Broadway.

"So what happened?" Our eyes meet as we wait for the streetlight to change. The first of March will make its long-awaited appearance in two days. With the sun readying for spring, closer now to our tiny spot on the planet than it's been for months, it bears down, giving Cameron's blue-green eyes a touch of glitter.

"Kayla and Chelsea happened. They stopped me in the bathroom to tell me my sister's a whore and she's been messing around with Scott."

Cameron leads me across the busy street. "Hooking up with Scott doesn't make your sister a whore. It makes her a girl with bad taste in men, but not a whore."

"They said she'd be sorry if she didn't stop. To be honest, and this is part of what makes me so damn mad, I hope they do teach her a lesson!" I free my hand from Cameron's, stopping to lean against a tall brick building. "I mean, I don't care who Missy dates or hooks up with, but she's making our lives hell. Ever since that night, remember, the night *Oklahoma!* opened and I—" I look down at the pavement.

"What? Fell for a handsome, talented, soon-to-be world famous director?"

I blush as Cameron puts his hands around my waist. "Quit it. This is serious. I'm being serious."

Cameron nods, fingering his chin.

"It's just that my whole life has been about taking care of someone else. If it wasn't Mom, it was Grace, who, yeah, I realize didn't turn out so normal, but I did my best. That was my life, but now it's different. I don't even know where my mother is, but, like Grandma says, it's not my responsibility. She's not my responsibility, and Grace – she's got Grandma to look after her now. This is the first time I've been free to think about myself, and Missy... well, I know she's not doing it on purpose, but she's fucking it up!"

Cameron takes my hand, guiding me along. "I wish I could tell you what to do, but I don't really know what this is like because I don't have brothers or sisters. When my parents split and my mom moved to California, I definitely blamed myself. I didn't realize how much they hated each other because they kept that secret from me. I thought if I'd known I could have done something... I don't know; brought them back together somehow, but I've realized that it wasn't my job, just like it's not your job to take care of your mother. I don't know what to say about Missy, but I would say you have a choice." Halfway to Riverside Drive, Cameron stops. "Either you treat Missy's problem like it's your own and spend all your free time watching everything she does and, I don't know, reporting back to your grandma like you were some private detective from one of those old movies, or you live your life, and let Missy live hers. She's old enough to make her own decisions."

"And if something happens?" I cross my arms, looking in the opposite direction as the cars race by. "If Missy gets hurt? Or if, like I heard Grandma say to Grandpa the other night, she's got a bipolar disorder too, then what? She is my younger sister."

"I really don't know, Bri. I don't know what to say about that. I still don't think it's your job to take care of everyone in your family while you're in high school. That just seems screwed up to me."

Holding hands, we make our way into the park.

~~~~

"So this is where you come, then. This is that special spot."

"Uh-huh." I tie my hair in a ponytail to keep it from blowing in two directions as the wind sweeps through from the north and the cars, zooming past the highway, create a competing breeze of their own, their engines full throttle. Staring out at the Hudson, I try to conjure the image I always have. I search for a glimpse of that ghost of myself, the one who can never swim past the river's middle to reach the other side, but she is nowhere in sight.

"I can see why you like it." Cameron spins around, stopping to inspect the gated-off skateboard rink. "I've never been down here but, when I was in eighth grade, I would've jumped that fence, for sure. You'd have to pry me off those ramps."

Turning back to the water, I open my mouth, ready to tell Cameron about the daydream I have whenever I'm here alone.

He stops me before I begin. "What was he like? Your father, I mean. You never really say much about him."

A slight heaviness, like the kind you feel when slipping on a life vest, presses down on my shoulders. The weight lingers a moment, then disappears.

"He…" Craning my neck, I catch a glimpse of the George Washington Bridge, that destination most cars speeding by are headed for. "He was kind." My response surprises me. I can't remember ever using the word kind to describe anyone. It is a pretty word, though. I make a mental note to use it again. "He didn't talk much, but when he did you'd want to be quiet and listen. He…" I close my eyes to get a better picture. "He was pretty tall; at least that's how I remember him. To me, he always seemed tall and sturdy, and he was pale. Mom used to say he had skin like a linen tablecloth. I remember because I'd go around examining tablecloths, trying to find one that resembled my dad. I—" I smile at the memory. "I didn't get that she was exaggerating."

"I bet she'd say that about me," Cameron chuckles.

"Probably. I guess… well, Dad was sort of handsome. He wasn't like one of those heart-stopping movie stars or anything. Mom could've easily married one of those, but I'm glad she didn't. I'm glad—"

"Can I ask," Cameron's blushes then lays his hand on my shoulder. "How did he die?"

I turn, my face just inches from his. There's a faded freckle on the tip of his nose. I'd never noticed it before. "He died in a car accident." I rest my back against the iron gate separating Riverside Park from the highway. Wheels spinning about fifty miles per hour down the black tar-paved strip sound louder than ever. "He and Mom had a fight. I remember Missy and I were watching a movie in the living room: *The Wizard of Oz*. We were at that part where they all fall asleep in a field of poppies. Mom came out of the kitchen. She sat on the couch between Missy and me – she had a pretty looking drink in her hand. It was blue like those flat-faced lollipops your doctor gives you after a round of shots, I remember thinking. She was all giggly, trying to play around. She started tickling Missy. Missy put out her arm; I guess Mom was blocking her view. She knocked Mom's hand and the drink spilled over.

'You'—" I look down at the dirt ground. Tiny blades, like adolescent stubble, poke through the top layer. I think about growth, focus on the lifespan of the grass beneath my sneakers as I continue. "'You little shit!' Mom jumped up. She slapped Missy across the face. Missy started crying, and that's when Dad came downstairs. He held Missy, kissed her, told her it was okay then took Mom by the arm into the kitchen. They started arguing. I turned up the volume on the TV to drown out their yelling. Something crashed in the kitchen and shattered. Mom kicked the kitchen door open. She hit the button on the TV and told us to go upstairs immediately. I took Missy's hand and we ran up. We lay on our bellies on the second floor landing to see what would happen. Missy huddled next to me. 'Mom's hitting everything today,' she whispered. I told her to keep quiet. Dad came out and Mom told him to leave. 'I don't love you anymore, get out!' she said. He didn't argue, didn't tell her how he loved her or how she didn't mean what she was saying. He just called for us to come down. Missy got up, made it halfway down the stairs, but Mom came, stood in front of the first step with her arms out so Missy couldn't get by. 'Just get out,' she yelled."

As I speak, revisiting the scene, those moments before the accident that changed my... our lives forever, all I can think is, *this isn't my voice*. I mean yes, I know it's me telling the story, but it doesn't feel like me. It's more like someone recorded my voice, learned my story, then somehow had the recording tell it for me. I'm empty of feeling. I could be rattling off a list for a grocery store run; it's all dead-tone and automatic. A rusty old car has more expression than I, standing, my back to a roaring speedway, telling my first-ever boyfriend about the last time I saw my father.

Without warning, Cameron puts his arms around me. I let my head rest on his shoulder, my upper body sinking into his. Pulling back, taking my face in his hands, Cameron tilts his head.

"What—?" I begin.

"It's like this." His lips press against mine, not unlike the pecks we've exchanged since the night of *Oklahoma!* but as the pressure intensifies, I open my mouth.

His tongue tastes salty, perhaps from whatever he last ate. His chin feels prickly against my smooth cheek. His lips are chapped from the cold, almost-March afternoon, but with these tiny discomforts, in spite of them, a long thrill ripples through me, reaching the top of my head and the tips of my toes all at once. My fingers stretched wide, I cup my hands around Cameron's head. Short hay-colored wisps tickle the crevices between each finger, and I tilt my head, first to the left, then the right. I follow his movements, as though caught in an unfamiliar dance, but I catch on quick. Within seconds, it's me leading each embrace, each caress, and I wonder, taking a moment to look back at the cars zipping by, if this is what it's all about – this feeling of willingly losing myself, because if it is, then I've misread all the stories, misunderstood every tale. Here, at the very bottom of Riverside Park, is the scene – a short story – of two bodies, two teenagers, connecting.

Cameron's hand in mine, we start onward, leaving the budding plants and unclothed trees to watch over cars speeding by the Hudson. Halfway up the stone steps, I turn back one last time and, for a flicker of a moment, see a figure – brown hair, olive skin and a black one-piece – gliding past the river's midway point. From where I stand, her breaststroke looks steady. This time I feel confident she will make it to the other side.

Chapter Ten

I'll be seventeen in exactly one month. *March 3, 2009*, I write at the top of my new journal entry. *Things to accomplish before April 3rd*:

Bring math grade up to at least a C-

Be kinder to Missy, even if she's rude as hell

Finish reading Wuthering Heights, *even though I hate Cathy*

Spend more time with Grandma, Grandpa and Grace

Buy a dress to wear to birthday dinner with Cameron

Stop being so obsessed with kissing and consider that other thing Cameron talked about

Find Mom

My back to the elevator wall, journal in hand, I head down to the basement. While I'm pretty sure using the theater as a private space for writing and reading isn't allowed, I don't see where else I can sit in peace during this forty-five minute break. Cameron's busy in math class, so I'm by myself for now – not such a bad thing, since I have a lot to figure out.

The doors rattle, opening on a scene of twelve-or-so bodies facing the entrance to the theater. As I step out, I notice a sheet pasted to the wall. Shuffling past a cluster of students, I see Skylar and Aaron holding hands, staring up at the notice.

Spring play announcement:

Because *Oklahoma!* was such a great success, we have decided our actors are ready for a challenge! This spring's play will be Tennessee Williams' *A Streetcar Named Desire*. All those interested, please see Mr Shaffer, fifth floor, homeroom 11A. Because of the sensitive nature of this play, a signed consent form <u>will</u> be required from parents/guardians of <u>all</u> those who wish to participate. Auditions begin March 10th.

"Isn't that the one about the crazy chick who visits her sister and gets carted off to a mental institution?" an unfamiliar male voice from behind me asks.

"I think so, though she's kind of normal at first, right? Then her sister's husband screws around with her," another voice, female, replies.

"Right. She goes crazy after he rapes her. How the hell are we gonna do that?"

"I don't think the rape happens on stage, but yeah, holy shit! That'll be intense."

Making for the stairwell at the other end of the hall, a gazillion thoughts rush through my head. I look over the flyer one last time – *Auditions begin March 10th*; the words seem to spring out like the title on a 3D movie – then I kick into a jog.

Once behind the heavy blue door, I plop down, my

journal falling from my hands, its loose contents scattering before me. "God has one strange sense of humor." Grandpa's statement from the night before reenters my mind like an old song. A news show about a woman in a poor town in Russia, who illegally sold her youngest daughter to a couple from the States so she could feed her other five children, captivated us. Three months later the woman's estranged uncle died, leaving her a small fortune. On television, she sent out a plea to the American family to return her daughter. "Terrible, terrible fate," Grandpa shook his head. "God has no pity."

"Watch what you say, Kalman." Grandma swatted the TV switch. "That woman abandoned her little girl. She deserves no pity now, just because she's come into some money. If you can't care for children, you don't have them in the first place."

Grandma's harsh words surprised me, but more than that, I considered Grandpa's response. God: I imagined a muscular man carrying a golden staff, his hair the color of unused cotton, slapping his knee and roaring like a drunkard as he watches pain and suffering from atop a cloud. I consider the image again, now. I know my circumstances are different. Compared to the woman who sold her daughter, I live a perfect life. I just can't believe that the school I am in, because my mother dropped me off in another state when she couldn't be bothered to look after my sisters and me, would randomly decide to put on a play... the very play Mom did years ago before turning into something awful – someone who, just a few months later, sat stone-faced at her husband's funeral then never stepped foot on a stage again. I can't believe such a thing could happen for no reason.

Sitting on the gray steps littered with scuff marks and dust clumps, I extend my arms and imagine two possibilities, one cupped in each palm. Either God is playing a game, toying with me by having Whitman Prep put on a production of the play that marked the end of my mostly solid childhood, or he's trying to give me a chance at something special – something I can't know yet. Either way, I decide, bending over to collect the scraps on the floor, I will try out. I'll audition for the role of Blanche, and maybe I'll get it. Maybe I'll play that 'crazy chick who gets carted off to a mental institution.' Who knows? I might just find that one special thing I'm meant to do. Perhaps I was born to act.

~ ~ ~ ~

"Hey!" Cameron greets me outside Mr Shaffer's classroom. "Came to say hi?"

I pull him aside, letting a group of students – that eager-to-be- done-with- math-class look smeared across their faces – pass by. "I'm gonna try out."

"For the Yankees? No offence, Bri, but I don't think they take—"

"For Blanche. For Blanche in *Streetcar*."

Cameron cocks his head, squinting as he studies my expression, like he can't tell if I'm serious. I stifle my irritation.

"When did you decide that?"

"Just now. I went down to the basement to do some stuff, and I saw the flyer. I can do it, Cam. I can play Blanche."

"I never said you couldn't. It's just—"

"What?" I stamp. "Just what?"

"Just maybe it's not such a great idea."

Steaming blood springs to my cheeks as I recall those years I spent reading lines with Mom past midnight. I watched scenes over and over so Mom could teach me what makes one moment an acting gem in cinematic history. All that yet my boyfriend thinks I can't get the lead role in some gimpy high school production.

"I don't care what you think." I push past Cameron, his brows raised and mouth wide open like a child who's not sure whether to explain himself or cower, and charge through the open classroom door.

Next to the equation-filled chalkboard, a sign hangs above a left-handed desk. *Streetcar Info*, the notice reads. Looking back, I half expect to see Cameron pouting in the doorway, but he's nowhere in sight. Two stacks lay close together on the desktop: *Permission Slip* and *Audition Sign-up Sheet*. I carefully pen my name in one of the March tenth slots: *Sabrina Marie Gibbons*. If I'm ever a real actress, I'll use my full name. Why not begin now? I stick a permission slip in my knapsack.

"Under the desk," a deep voice from behind me urges.

"Huh?" I turn to face Aaron. "What—?"

"The scripts – they're on the chair below the desk." He points to a stack of playbooks. Taking one from the pile, I hold it up, running my fingers over the photograph on the cover: Vivien Leigh. I'd know her face anywhere, but here she doesn't have that expression of self-assurance, that calculating stare she wears so beautifully as Scarlett O'Hara. Here she seems lost, almost haggard. A recent memory of Mom hunched over the kitchen table after a fight with Jim visits me like a phantom. Grace and I'd just come in from outdoors. We'd been playing with the neighbor's Dalmatian who, regardless of the weather, always remained tied to a tree in their yard. Mom's swollen eye and the shattered glass in the corner were enough to tell the story – one repeated so often it'd begun to wear a duffle bag with the word *Cliché* written in sprawling letters in place of a logo. I think back, now, to the look on Mom's face – desperation mixed with bewilderment. 'How the hell did I get here,' her eyes seemed to ask as she turned to face me and Grace. 'How?'

"Who're you trying out for?" Like a thunder crackle, Aaron's voice jolts me back into the present moment.

"Huh?" I shift around then quickly look down at the book in my hand. The memory ghost is gone. "Blanche." I step aside so Aaron can sign up and collect his script.

"Oh?"

"Yeah. What about you?"

"Stanley, of course." Aaron sticks the playbook in his bag. "You're gonna have some fierce competition, you know." He eyes me. "Sky's got her heart set on playing Blanche, and she's pretty damn good."

"Well—" I begin.

"Have you thought about going out for Stella?" Aaron interrupts before I can finish. "To be honest, don't tell Sky I told you this, but I've always thought Stella was the better role. I mean, she does kinda hold the play together."

"Does Skylar have you talk everyone out of auditioning for the roles she wants?"

"No, I'm not Sky's watchdog." Aaron raises his chin, crosses his arms. "I just… forget it. Do what you want."

"I will," I call as Aaron makes a dash for the door.

Readying to head to my next class, I notice Mr Shaffer standing still, watching me. He opens his mouth as though he's about to say something when a cluster of students surge through the door. Led by Kayla, the chatty mob settles, each body finding a desk to plop down in – each, except for Kayla who, swiveling her hips, moseys up to Mr Shaffer. "I have a note from my mother," she exclaims. "I will have to take the test next week."

"I'll only accept a note from a doctor. You know that."

"My father's a doctor – a surgeon. Will you accept a letter from him, then?"

"Please find a seat, Kayla. We can talk about this after class."

"Fine." As she swerves, catching a glimpse of me in the corner, Kayla leers, her eyes like blue fire. She motions toward Scott, who, sitting off to the side, is clearly oblivious to anything going on. I can't believe Missy's interested in him! Then, her left brow raised, she mouths watch it. I gather my belongings at rapid speed and dart out, forgetting to close the door behind me.

~~~~

Over the past few weeks I've begun to rearrange Mom's old room to better fit my style. In place of the poster of Audrey Hepburn as *Sabrina* – linking arms with two goofy looking men, one on each side – I've hung a square bulletin board. The old polaroid of Mom at the sea sits tacked in the middle, surrounded by postcards, pictures and printed sheets with sayings on them. In English class we read a poem by Emily Dickinson:

The soul selects her own Society,
Then shuts the door;
On her divine majority
Obtrude no more.

Unmoved, she notes the chariot's pausing
At her low gate;
Unmoved, an emperor is kneeling
Upon her mat.

I've known her from an ample nation—
Choose one;
Then close the valves of her attention
Like stone.

Grandma teared up when I read it to her. "Makes me think of home," she sighed. "Remind me to teach you some of our people's poetry one of these days. Mrs Dickinson is beautiful, yes, but nothing touches the soul like the poetry of one's own ancestors."

Still, I tore the page out of my copy of *Great American Poets* and hung it above the photo of Mom. For me, each time I enter the room and look up at

Dickinson's words, I imagine my head – skin surrounding a thick, white skull that protects my most valuable organ. At the very center, the midpoint of my mind, I envision a castle set upon a river. As water moves freely, this way and that, sometimes rippling over an entranceway that extends to dry land like a long stone tongue, the castle remains firmly anchored, still in its place. At the front of the castle, a blue door, like a garage door, hangs above the entrance. People I've known throughout my almost seventeen years of life line up, waiting to see who will be admitted and who cast out. The first to step through, and they do so together, holding hands, are Grandma and Grace. Next, grinning like a proud warrior, his head up high, Cameron enters. After Cameron, I admit the ghost of my father, his form wavering slightly with each gust of wind. Grandpa comes next, hesitant as though he's uncomfortable heading into unknown territory. The door lowers a bit as Missy walks up, her arms crossed, looking around like she's afraid someone might see. 'Is walking into a castle something a cool person would do?' she likely wonders, but comes in all the same. Jim is next in line. With a heavy thump, the door falls like the blade on a guillotine. As he turns away, he's threatened, given a ten-second warning by my mind's castle guard. "Away with you!" the guard bellows. "The punishment for loitering is death!" Mom arrives last, after a cluster of others have either been given permission or turned away. She is cloaked in her favorite leopard print fur coat. Halfway up the stone path, she stops. I instruct the castle guard to go to her at once. He pulls her aside, whispering something I can't hear. Mom shakes her head, staring down at the ground.

Extending his arm, the guard tries once more, pointing to the open door, but it's no use. Mom turns for a brief moment to wave then starts back down the path. The clatter of her black heels grows faint. Her figure shrinks with each stride and I know, watching the top of her head until it is completely overshadowed by trees and thick foliage, she will not be back. Not again. Not at my door.

With my new bulletin board on a thin wire above me, I sit knees up on the floor and go over my scene for tomorrow's audition. I've chosen a segment from the beginning of the play. Blanche has just arrived in New Orleans from Mississippi. She's dressed all in white. A woman points her in the direction of the home of her sister, Stella, and new brother-in-law, Stanley. In Stella's kitchen, Blanche sees an open whiskey bottle and rushes toward it. She pours a drink then tosses it in the sink, deciding to remain sober, if she can stand it. Stella arrives, and Blanche springs to embrace her. This is where I've chosen to begin, the very moment Blanche lays eyes on her younger sister. As I ready to begin, there's a tiny tapping on my door. "I'm practicing my lines," I call out. Grace turns the knob, peeps through, then shuffles in.

"Can I watch?" She holds Daisy Girl to her chest.

"Why don't you go sit with Grandma? I bet she'll tell you a story if you ask."

"No." Grace shakes her head wildly. Brown strands are strewn across her cheeks when she's finished. "She's in the kitchen with Grandpa. They're talking in that language again. I don't know what they're saying."

"Well, I can't play with you now. I'm practicing for tomorrow." I lay the playbook down, my index finger holding my place.

"I know. I can just watch."

Before I have a chance to protest, Grace scuttles across the room, plopping down next to me. I return to my lines.

Blanche begins, talking quickly, like she's so nervous she might explode. Stella's the calm one, the anchor. She listens, unbothered that her sister barely gives her a chance to speak. I start, reading both Blanche and Stella's lines. It'd be great if I had someone to practice with. If only Missy wasn't such a jerk these days.

"Can I help?" Grace taps my knee.

"Huh?" I look up. "Help with what?"

"With that." Grace points to the play. "I read good now," she grins.

"Well. It's I read well; not good. This is grown-up reading. It's not for you."

"I read grown-up books too, you know. I read *The Hobbit*—"

"No, Grandma read *The Hobbit* to you."

"Well, I read some of the words. What's this about, anyways?" Grace pokes *Streetcar*, almost knocking it out of my hands. "Why's it so grown-uppy?"

I lay the playbook down again. It's clear I won't get much done with Grace asking a question every few seconds. I turn, crossing my legs, to face my youngest sister. She mimics my movement, placing Daisy Girl in the small space between us.

"It's about two sisters," I begin.

"Is it real?" Grace interrupts. "Did it actually happen?"

"No. It's made-up, like *The Hobbit*."

Grace nods in understanding.

"One sister's name is Blanche and the other is Stella. Blanche is the big sister, but they're grown-up, not kids or teenagers. When they were young, they lived in a large house in Mississippi with lots of space to run around. It was a plantation. The people who took care of Stella and Blanche grew older, just like Stella and Blanche did, because no one can stay young forever, right?"

Her eyes as wide as a baby starling's mouth during feeding time, Grace bobs her head. "Right," she agrees.

"Well, Stella moved away from Mississippi, to a place called New Orleans. She's the sweet sister – sensitive and caring. She didn't want to leave Blanche and her family all alone but felt she had to. She had to start her own life, so she did. She moved away and got married. Blanche stayed in Mississippi and watched the people she loved grow old and die. She had to sell the land – all that space she and Stella used to run around and play on when they were little girls – to pay for the funerals. When everyone was dead and the home and land were sold, Blanche had no place to go. The play begins when she moves to New Orleans to live with Stella and Stella's husband, Stanley." Hoping that will be enough to satisfy Grace's curiosity, I pick my playbook back up and open to where I left off.

"Is Blanche mad?" Grace pulls on my shirtsleeve. "Is she mad that she got left behind?"

"Well..." I place the book back on the wooden floor. "She's more... I don't know what the word is, really. She's nervous – like every little thing is too much after all she's been through."

"Then what happens?"

"Stella wants to take care of her big sister. She feels bad that Blanche had to sell the house and watch everyone die, so she lets Blanche live with her for a little while. That's when all the trouble starts."

Grace lies on her stomach, her feet up in the air. "Does Blanche make trouble?"

"She doesn't fit in with Stella and Stanley. Stella's pregnant so she has a lot to get ready for – expecting a baby and all – and Stanley; he's a bad person, a jerk like Ji—" I stop before the whole name slips out, but Grace catches on. Narrowing her eyes, she sits up.

"Like Daddy, you mean." She folds her arms.

I shrug, laying my hand on the play. I wonder if I can manage that look of desperation Vivien Leigh wears on the cover. Before I have time to answer, decide in a fraction of a moment whether to be honest or try to change the subject, Grandma barges in.

"Ah!" She sighs, letting her hands drop. "I've been looking everywhere for you."

"I was just talking to Bri." Grace gets up, scooping Daisy Girl into her arms like a mother would a newborn.

"It's past ten o'clock! Let's go. Into the bathroom and brush your teeth. Sabrina, I need you in the kitchen."

Before exiting, Grace turns back. "You'll be Stella, the sweet sister?"

I get up, sticking the play under my arm. "I want to play Blanche. Mom played Blanche once a long time ago."

Shaking her head, Grace shuffles through the open doorway. "I think you should be Stella. That's what I think." She disappears, Grandma close behind her.

Chapter Eleven

Grandpa wraps his knuckles on the wooden table, a copy of today's *New York Times* in front of him. He looks up as I stand, my back to the swinging doors, worn sacks of skin like small used tea bags, drooping beneath his gray eyes. With a complexion the color of a decade-old penny, dark copper and rugged, gray eyes and tufts of chestnut hair – it would have been lush like Mom's, years ago – he must have been gorgeous as a young man. I study him now: his sagging eyes, heavy jowls and the row of creases above his thick eyebrows. Age has left its mark on my grandfather. Age plus heartache, side-by-side like competitive running mates, yield something entirely different – worse.

Grandpa's lips stretch to form a half-smile. That seems about all he can manage. "Is there a possibility?" he begins, averting his eyes for a moment. "Do you think you might know where Marissa is?"

Taking a seat at the opposite side of the table, I shake my head. "She doesn't tell me anything." I consider mentioning Scott Shapiro, what Kayla and Chelsea told me about Missy hooking up with him, but decide against it. There's no way to know how much of what those two say is true.

"When your mo... my Sheila was young, like you two, she'd stay out like this. Grandma and I spent hours sitting at this very table, worried sick. I—" Grandpa looks toward the doors then lowers his voice. "I know girls like to have a good time; of course I know that, but things are different in a city like New York. A young girl can't just go out dancing in a club late at night. There's too much trouble. She can get hurt—taken advantage of. When Sheila was a girl, I should have taken more of a stand. I regret that more than anything else in my life." Grandpa rests his chin on a closed-tight fist. "Discipline," he continues, his eyes locked onto mine. "Like the Germans say – their word for it escapes me now, but it was the one thing that country ever understood correctly – discipline. It's something a father should instill in his daughters most of all. You see, I never believed in those hospitals, Sabrina – the doctors, that nonsense they gave us about medications, disorders, and for what? To keep a girl from having spirit? It's always a diagnosis in this country, always something to be cured with a little round pill. No." Grandpa brings his fist down on the table. "Discipline! A girl should have spirit, but it must be contained. The answer is discipline and, for a daughter, it must come from her father."

"Missy doesn't have a father." I turn my head quickly, frightened by my grandfather's piercing glare. In all the years I've known him, I've never seen this side – the side that takes a stand and, in so many words, lets it be known. He's always been the quiet one, the one who silently judges.

"That's the problem. No father is the problem."

"I don't think so." Placing *A Streetcar Named Desire* on the table, I look straight into the seawater gray of Grandpa's eyes. "I don't have a father anymore either, but I'm not running around, doing whatever I want, worrying everyone. Missy just wants attention. She's selfish and too damn smart for anyone to beat her at her own little game. If I stayed out and got drunk and stoned all the time, never getting a chance to study, I'd get thrown out of school. There'd be real consequences, but Missy won't have that, no matter what. Instead, she'll be the star math student, probably get an award or something, and the whole time she'll be laughing because she won. She won at her own stupid game of doing whatever she wants and getting away with it."

"I don't know." Grandpa gets up, moving toward the stove. He flips the knob, setting blue and orange flames free to dance, wild but still contained beneath the teakettle.

Accompanied by a rustle of wind, Grandma pushes through the doors. Transparent waves of air excite the fire and it rises, threatening to claim more than its skimpy spot on the stove, but without sufficient room, surrounded on all sides by thick black metal, it settles down, defeated, forced to burn steadily in its confined space.

"It's eleven thirty, Kal. I'm calling the police." Grandma reaches for the portable phone on counter's edge.

"No!" Grandpa lunges, grabbing the phone then hiding it behind his back. I try not to laugh as he reminds me of a child who can't stand to hand over his precious toy.

"Where's Marissa?" Grandma glares at me.

Giving a start, I gasp, surprised by what seems like anger directed my way. "How should I know?"

"You're her older sister! You don't have any idea at all where she might be?"

"No!" I get up, kicking my chair from under me. "Missy's a brat. Don't you two see that? She wants this kind of attention! She wants everyone to be freaking out, obsessing over where she is. All this panic is giving her what she wants!" Grabbing my playbook, I rush toward the doors. "She's gonna keep this up, you know. You're just feeding into what she wants!" In a rage, I storm through the hallway, slamming my door behind me once I reach the bedroom.

With Grandma and Grandpa still in the kitchen, each on the verge of giving the other a heart attack, I settle back on the floor, my bulletin board stable above me.

Reaching up, I run my fingers across the bottom of the board's wooden frame. I look up at my photo of Mom, resting peacefully below Emily Dickinson's poem. *Where are you?* I ask. The empty room gives no answer.

~ ~ ~ ~

I must have dozed off for half an hour or so. A trickle of drool, moving at a slug's pace, makes its way down one side on my chin. Wiping my face, I stand. A sensation – like that moment in a movie when you know the murderer's about to strike, his knife in the air inches above his victim's chest – slithers, making its way throughout my skeleton. My fingers tingle as I reach for the doorknob. Down the hallway, I head toward Missy's room; it's the only one with the light still on. Her face to the wall, Missy lays curled on the bed. Grandma sits, statue-still, at her side.

"So she came back," I sneer, proud for the last time that I was right about my sister. She came back – must have gotten bored.

Grandma looks up, her eyes wide, glazed with a thick layer of fury. She rises quickly and I jump back, afraid she may smack me.

"What?" I ask, my heart ticking like a metronome that's been turned up to quadruple speed. The front buzzer rings and Grandma rushes past me. "What—?" I move to the edge of Missy's bed. Springs creak as she turns to face me, and I drop to my knees. I take it in in pieces, like examining a three-story tapestry, because there's no other way – no way to look at the bloodied lip, the enlarged nostril with gauze that has begun to take on a deep velvet red, and the left eye, too swollen to open.

"What happened?" I begin to sob, covering my mouth.

"I fucked up, Bri," Missy whispers. "This time I really fucked up."

"This way." Grandma leads two women, each in plain clothing, into the bedroom. "I changed her clothes. What she was wearing, it's all in that bag over there."

"You didn't wash any of it?" one of the women asks, lifting the tied up trash bag.

"No. The officer on the phone told me not to."

"That's really good; you've done everything right." The woman, speaking in a hushed voice, puts her hand on Grandma's shoulder then leads her out of the room.

The other lady, tall with freckles and reddish-brown hair bends down to Missy's eye level. "There are two men from the hospital. They're outside the apartment. They are safe, and they will not harm you. Your grandfather is with them now, and he'll stay by your side. You are safe now. Will you be alright if they come in here to take you to the hospital?"

Missy looks up at me standing by the bedpost. I've almost begun to believe I am invisible. Perhaps I wish it, too – invisible and cursed, my mouth sown shut for all the things I said about my sister.

"I want Bri to come," she murmurs.

The lady turns to face me, her bottle-green eyes greeting mine for the first time. "Are you Marissa's sister?"

I nod.

"I'll only go if she comes." Missy props herself up with her arms, then bends forward, balancing onto her bare feet. The effort seems draining, but she wrestles through it all the same.

The lady and I rush to grab Missy's arm as she doubles over, her hand pressed to her lower stomach, but she shakes us off. "I can walk. It's not so bad." Then, steadying her upper body, she reaches out and takes my hand. Together we walk through the open bedroom door and down the front hallway to where the men wait outside.

"She shouldn't be walking," one man says, pointing to a stretcher as we exit the apartment.

"I'm not getting on that thing," Missy hisses. I

tighten my grasp, adding my other hand, but not for physical support, because if it were possible to walk with absolutely no strength at all, my sister would be the one to do it.

~ ~ ~ ~

March 10, 2009: If I had a history book all to myself, that date would deserve an entire chapter. I make my way to school even though Grandma, after I left Missy asleep at the hospital –flying through dreamland thanks to the medication they gave her – said I could take the day to stay home and calm down. Rounding the corner, Whitman Prep's candy blue doors in plain view, I hear two voices, each turning to a whisper as the speakers near me. Chelsea is immediately recognizable; the nasal drone and drawn out syllables could make a person pray for deafness. Though she looks familiar, I don't know the name of the girl with her.

"How's your sister?" Chelsea asks as the two pass me on the sidewalk.

"What?"

The girls snigger. "I'm just asking how your sister is." Chelsea cocks her head and narrows her pale eyes, a look of victory smeared across her cold face.

"She's fine."

"Really?" Chelsea grins. "Because that's not what I heard."

I stop, a chill rattling my chest and shoulders as the two speed toward the school entrance. It ripples, as realizations sometimes do before making their way into full consciousness, then settles over me like a heavy quilt: one with violent images embroidered into each square. The auburn-haired lady from the Special Victims Unit asked, as Missy lay silent on her hospital bed, 'do you know who attacked you?' Missy, stone-faced, stared up at the too-bright ceiling. She wouldn't say one word.

~~~~

"Your grandmother already called me." Ms DeSousa shakes her head, the same purple rimmed glasses she wore on our first day enlarging her eyes, making them bulge in a grotesque manner. "I'm very sorry to hear about what happened to your sister." Something in her voice, the monotone carriage of each word, makes her response sound rehearsed – lines memorized by an unfeeling actress auditioning for a play.

I clear my throat. "I want to report something that happened – something that makes me think I know who was involved."

"If you think you know who injured your sister, you should tell the police. Ms DeSousa gets up, causally rearranging her desk – we could be carrying on a conversation about the start of a baseball season. "From what I heard, Marissa hasn't named anyone. I told your grandmother this, but I'll repeat it to you as well. The law is quite simple. You cannot prosecute an unnamed assailant. As I see it," she sits back, staring into the center of my eyes like a hypnotist. "There is no evidence that anyone here at Walt Whitman Preparatory, a school from which students carry on to places like Harvard and Duke, a school that, quite frankly has bent over backwards for you girls, was involved. Please just think, in all honesty, how many places would take in three new students mid-year? Three who, I'll be perfectly honest, wouldn't have had a chance of getting in through our usual admissions process. Most schools wouldn't, not here in New York City."

"But," I begin, my eyes burning, a feeling of shame resting on me like a thick layer of wet sand.

"Let me finish. We have bent over backward for you girls because we believe unpleasant circumstances in your lives should not hold you back from a promising future, so, Sabrina, think about that before you try to destroy this school's reputation by accusing one of our students of a heinous crime."

Before I can respond, Ms DeSousa puts the telephone receiver to her ear. "Please," she motions to the exit. "I have a lot of work to do."

Through the dark grey hallway, I trudge toward the elevator. Like Jane Eyre when she flees Thornfield after discovering Mr Rochester's secret, I feel cast off with no place to turn. I could go see the principal, Mr... I don't even know his name, but he'd likely say the same thing Ms DeSousa, with her fat pinched face and extra-terrestrial eyes, repeated. Chelsea clearly knows something. That, plus Kayla's threatening words should at least warrant an investigation. I can see all three of them – Kayla, Chelsea and Scott – concocting a plan: how to ruin the new, small-town tenth grader's life in just one night, and for what? To look cool? To feel powerful? If only Missy would talk, just tell somebody what happened! Can it be my place to go around making assumptions, however plausible they may be, accusing fellow students without knowing for sure what went on? What if I am wrong? Whitman Prep would be sure to throw us out, all three of us. Grace, without any idea of what went wrong, would be let down once again. I think of her, two fingers in her mouth, taking in the information – 'you can no longer go to Whitman Prep' – with a resigned nod, just like when it turned midnight and, after an entire day of waiting by the phone, she heard the words 'Momma's not calling, but I'm sure she remembers it was your birthday.' Waiting for the elevator, I long for Cameron's advice, or to even just hear his soothing voice.

"Hey, good luck today," a familiar voice breaks through my thought pattern like a drill pushing its way into a jammed keyhole.

I turn. "Huh?"

"You try out today, right?" Skylar smacks the elevator button. "Piece of crap," she mutters, pushing the button three more times.

The play! Shit, I'd completely forgotten. "Yeah, yes, yes today," I stutter.

"Well, good luck," she repeats. "Or break a leg, I guess."

Looking at my wristwatch, I notice it's already 9:30. I've only got fifteen minutes to prepare. What idiot chooses to audition at 9:45 in the morning? One who doesn't anticipate a sleep-robbing crisis the night before, I guess; one with a life very different from mine.

~ ~ ~ ~

From outside the theater I hear Mr Shaffer and

Cameron talking, getting ready for the first audition, which will be me. Cameron made it clear that the final decision would in no way affect our relationship. He had me promise not to break things off if I didn't get the part. "The decision will be made by me and Mr Shaffer. It's strictly business," he had declared. I'd laughed quietly to myself. The seriousness with which he considers his role as student director struck me as both adorable and funny at the same time. This morning, it's difficult to find amusement in anything.

Observing the second hand on my watch, I consider calling the whole thing off. I'd loved the idea of Grace, Grandma, Grandpa and Missy coming to watch me play Blanche DuBois, a role Mom mastered almost a decade earlier. Grace, having never seen live theater before, would be giddy with excitement. Missy, I knew, would feel embarrassed that her sister had become a theater geek, but Grandma would've made her come all the same. Thinking about her now, lying in the hospital room remembering, reliving God knows what, I begin to tremble. My chest seems to crumble inward, closing off all my airways. I kneel down, my back straight against the wall, and suck in. The tears come first, followed by a bout of dry coughing. A heavy thrust of the theater doors precedes the percussion of pattering feet.

"Oh my god! Bri, are you okay?" Cameron rushes to my side. "What happened? Is it... this isn't performance jitters, is it?" The panicked look, wrinkled forehead and bulging eyes let me know Cameron understands; he gets me enough to sense that I am struggling with more than just performance jitters. Mr Shaffer arrives, his foot acting as a doorstop. "Is everything alright?" He pokes his head out like a cautious turtle surveying its surroundings.

"I've got it," Cameron nods. The door slams shut.

"Missy," I heave, wiping my face with the back of my arm. "She came home last night, beaten... I... she wouldn't say anything but... I think she was raped." I whisper the last word as though a softer tone could make it less horrible.

"What?" Cameron shrieks.

"I don't know because she wouldn't say, but you should've seen her!" I grab the collar of Cameron's shirt for support. He doesn't flinch, though the sensation must be uncomfortable.

"What're you going to do?" Cameron takes my hand, sitting cross-legged on the cold basement floor. "How can I help?"

"I don't—"

Before I can finish, Mr Shaffer pokes his head back out, peering at us. I wonder if he's been standing by the door the entire time, listening. "Are you ready?" he asks.

Looking to my left I notice my knapsack has fallen over, its contents strewn across the floor. I must've been walking around with the zipper open all morning.

Packing it all in, notebooks, pencils, Mom's old copy of *Wuthering Heights*, I come, at last, to my journal. *The Sky's the Limit*, a dash with *old Spanish proverb* written in tiny letters below. The saying's been around for centuries, I imagine – long before Whitman Prep, *A Streetcar Named Desire*, all this, and us: me on the floor, Missy in the hospital, and Mom wherever she might be. Through harder times it has endured, existed on the backs of peoples' tongues, waiting to be uttered or even just considered. Closing my eyes, I repeat the words silently to myself. *The sky's the limit*. I wipe my face and, straightening my crinkled shirt, turn to Mr Shaffer. "I'm ready." The words come out cool and calm.

"Do you have your copy of the script?" he asks, ushering me into the dimly lit auditorium.

"I left it at home."

Cameron rushes to a table behind the last row of seats and hands me a playbook. I look at the front cover – the same as the one I've been studying at home, the image of Vivien Leigh, whose expression of desperation, loss of spirit and dignity I've been trying to emulate. *Acting comes from real life. It is the most honest job in the world*. Mom's words revisit me as I make my way down the narrow aisle to the black painted stage.

"You're trying out for Blanche?" Mr Shaffer calls from the second row as I climb three steps to stand under an all-revealing stage light.

I look once more at the playbook cover. "Stella," I reply. "I'd like to audition for Stella." Stella: the sweet sister, the naïve girl, the one who refuses to listen when Blanche needs her most.

Cameron, reading the lines of the other characters, accompanies me on stage. Together we enact the last scene, scene eleven, where Stella makes her decision. She chooses Stanley – a false sense of security – over her sister.

Chapter Twelve

Smooth and crisp, the March breeze brushes against my weary face. His hand in mine, Cameron accompanies me the short distance to the hospital. He doesn't initiate conversation, but when I mention that Grandma and Grandpa will likely be with Missy and, exhausted and overwhelmed, they may not give him much of a welcoming, Cameron stops, taking hold of my other hand.

Cameron pauses then looks directly into my eyes. "I don't know; I may be getting this all wrong, but they say the best actors pull from real life – that's what makes a great performer. With what you did this morning… well, Mr Shaffer and I may just announce that the role of Stella is taken because no one will throw themselves into that part the way you did this morning. There's no doubt, if you still want to, you will play Stella in this spring's production, but Bri, she isn't you."

Letting my hands drop, I stare down at the gritty

sidewalk. "Back in Butler we had a rule, Missy and I, though it was really mostly my rule." My eyelids grow heavy as I hang my head low, but I continue just the same. The sound of my voice ripples, each word held up by a separate gust of air. "There was a bus that stopped just down the road from our house… Mom and Jim's house. Sometimes when we'd go out, things would happen, things the three of us could never stop. Jim and Mom would fight or Mom would just lose it. If it got bad enough – the noise, violence, or Mom's weird behavior – if there were enough people around to see, someone would call the police. We could always tell. Missy was especially good at spotting the person off to the side, his cell phone pressed against his ear, looking over his shoulder every few seconds to take in and report on the commotion. We'd wait, but the moment the cops arrived, Missy and I would grab Grace and run to the nearest bus stop. I had a key to the house, and we'd let ourselves in, wait sometimes for hours, for somebody to come home. I'd heard stories about kids in foster homes. Jim said they were beaten, molested and even murdered. That's what he'd tell us. Once you got into a foster home, you didn't come out. I knew he was mostly full of shit, but I also knew from what I'd read at the library that siblings often ended up in different homes. I knew Grace for sure would be sent someplace different from me; Missy too, probably. I didn't want that. I didn't want us to be separated because then my whole world would be turned around. I never even went through Mom's things to find Grandma and Grandpa's number to call to let them know how bad things were because I thought they'd notify the authorities and have us sent some place too." I stop to take a deep breath. "I couldn't stand to leave my mother. No matter how bad things got. I knew, well... thought, anyways, that she'd never survive without me. Clearly I was wrong about that."

Cameron pauses, fingering his chin. I imagine his brain pumping full force, straining to take it all in, understand then respond in the best way possible. He bends forward, attempting to engage my stare. "You were just trying to protect everyone. How's that wrong?"

"It's just the opposite." I glance up. The sky has already begun to take on a deeper shade of blue. "I was selfish. I thought I was protecting everyone, but I was really just protecting myself... well, myself and Mom. I wasn't thinking about the people who really needed protecting. I was weak, like Stella. I let us all – my younger sisters – go on living in that horrible, disgusting house because of what I needed. I mean, what if we'd stayed during one of those public scenes when the police came? What if I went straight up and said, 'these are our parents and this is what we live with all the time?' Maybe then, years ago, our lives would have changed; Missy wouldn't hate herself and everyone else so damn much, and Grace wouldn't be totally fucked up like a three-year-old in an eight-year-old's body, though she is getting better now that she has Grandma. What if I'd taken a chance and let other people help us? Maybe then none of this would've happened. Maybe we'd have had a chance at being normal."

"Bri," Cameron takes my hand, leading me onward. "You should know by now, after spending this much time in the real world, that nobody's normal.

We're all freaks in our own little ways. That's why there are so many books, movies and plays. That's the whole point. There's no end to how fucked up normal people can be."

I smile for the first time since the night before. "I think my grandparents will like you." I put my arm around Cameron's shoulders.

"I hope so. What's that word you taught me – the one in Hungarian?"

"It's more than a word. It looks like just one word, but it's actually an entire phrase: *Szeretlek*, but if you tell my grandparents you love them already, they may think you're a bit weird."

"Well, it's like I told you; we're all a little strange."

"All freaks in our own little ways." I kiss Cameron's cheek as we reach the hospital entrance.

"All of us," he nods.

The sliding doors open. We step through.

~~~~

Third floor, Wing 101: the white hallway and grey linoleum floors add to an unsettling brightness. As we step into the waiting area, under a row of florescent lights, there's a sensation like the one you feel after attempting to stare into the sun. Blinding light: though I'd never really considered the phrase, it enters my mind as Cameron and I join my family, both of us cupping our hands over our eyes until the glare becomes tolerable.

Grace is the first to greet Cameron. She springs to her feet. "Are you Bri's friend?" she grins.

"I think so." Cameron pats the top of her head. "I'm definitely her boyfriend, but I think we're regular friends, too."

Grace giggles, her eyes two yellow balls of mischief. "Boyfriend." She shakes her head.

"Just sit back and be still." Grandma points to the empty chair on her right. Grace complies, still giggling.

"I'm Marta." Grandma extends a hand. "This is Kalman."

To my surprise, Cameron bows his head. A passerby might think he was addressing a queen. "It's a pleasure to meet you. You too, sir," he nods toward Grandpa. "I'm so sorry about Missy. If there's anything I can do to help, please let me know."

"That's very thoughtful, young man," Grandpa nods in return.

"If you'd like to take a seat," Grandma points to the chair next to Grace. "I'll make sure the little one doesn't bother you."

Cameron settles in. "I don't mind," he smiles. "I like kids."

"Sabrina," Grandma gestures for me to come closer. She switches to a whisper, clutching my arm. Her nails could use a trim. "Go see if you can talk some sense into her. They've run tests, we'll soon know more about..." She covers her mouth, raising one finger as she shakes herself back, returning to that tough, always composed woman my sisters and I have come to rely on. "You know." She clears her throat. "That lady from the Special Victims squad, Ms Rourke – I think Marissa likes her, but you know your sister. She's too damn stubborn to listen! Ms Rourke said the same thing that horrible woman at your school told me before giving some lecture on how students from Whitman go to great colleges, as though that makes a difference in this matter. I told her educated people can be as wicked as anybody else – just look at Stalin! – but all our hands are tied if Marissa says nothing. She knows who did this, Sabrina."

"I think so too," I agree, loosening my arm from Grandma's grip.

"Oh, I believe in my soul she knows. Please try. Get her to tell you." Our eyes lock and I see that look; the one I've tried to emulate for weeks now, practicing in the bathroom mirror, or in our kitchen window at night when the sky is dark enough to back a solid reflection – desperation, complete with nothing forceful enough to compete.

"I'll do my best."

Before entering Missy's hospital room, I turn back, look to Cameron, hoping for a supportive gesture, a glance that'll let me know everything will turn out all right. Instead he sits, fingering his chin, feigning interest, at least I imagine, as Grace shows him pictures in one of the books she's learning to read. I recognize the dark blue photograph on the front cover. It's the book she loves most, the one about dolphins, the one from which she has learned that the air-breathing sea creatures travel in packs, like happy families, and they never abandon one another, not even in the face of life-threatening danger.

~~~~

To my surprise, Missy smiles, propping herself up with an extra pillow, as I enter the small, square room.

In just a few hours her swollen eye has taken on a sullen purple, like a patch made of over-ripe grape skins. I stare at my shoes briefly, trying to gather the courage to take another look, this time without wanting to turn away.

"I look like shit, I know." Missy's voice is hoarse, raspy, reminding me of Bette Davis, the actress Mom could never come to like. It was the voice, she said – irritating as hell.

I point to a plastic tray next to Missy's bed. A round container of orange juice lays open but untouched.

She shakes her head. "I don't want anything right now."

Taking a seat next to Missy's bed, I look once more at my sneakers. In a perfect world, a sentence would appear like a cue card across one side of my shoe. It would vanish before Missy had a chance to roll over and see. One glance would be enough for me to know where to start, at what point to wade in so that, instead of fighting against me, the rough current could help move me along, carrying me to the perfect point of entry where I would take the plunge, hold my nose and dive into the murky deep.

"How do you feel?" The words come naturally as I greet my sister's stare.

"I kicked the nurse... this morning... so I feel kinda like an asshole." She turns to face the opposite wall.

"Why? What happened?"

"She came to give me an exam... down there." Missy points to *that* area. Her lower half is covered by a wool blanket making it look like the extra bedding was added for protection. It's as though someone thought the thick fabric could keep my sister safe from any additional harm. "They did the exam anyway, though," she sighs. "They gave me something to relax so I wouldn't break another nurse's face."

"Maybe—" I reach over to take Missy's hand then decide against it. Her arms lay soldier-still at her sides. She seems to be most comfortable that way. "I bet they've had that before. I bet you're not the only person who's tried to fight the exam lady."

"Maybe." Missy rolls onto her side. She eyes me suspiciously. "Are you also here to ask who messed with me last night?"

"No!" I look toward the door. An urge to get up and run stings my knees. I fight it, pressing the sides of my knees together until the impulse passes. "I wanted to see how you are, but I don't see why you won't tell if you know. It doesn't make sense. You're not winning by keeping quiet."

"This has nothing to do with winning or losing!" Bringing her fist down on the bedside, Missy sits up, her back perfectly straight. Cross-legged, she places the blanket on her lap. For some reason, I'd thought she could barely move but here, in front of me on her hospital bed, elevated and unbreakable like an Egyptian cat statue, Missy seems the healthier of the two of us. "I..." She looks to the door, then back. "You know what I was just thinking?" A glazed expression, like that of a lonesome kitten, shimmers across her face.

"No." I smile, looking up at her. The light caresses both cheekbones, what Mom referred to as Missy's patrician nose, and her black lashes just so, lending to a picturesque image. The scars and bruises will heal. Her beauty will remain untarnished, always. "I could never really read you, you know, even when we were little."

"I wish Mom were here." Pulling her knees up, she laughs one of those uncomfortable laughs. "I know she wouldn't be able to make this all go away. That was never her job anyway. Dad was always the one to kiss us when we got hurt."

"I remember." I clench my fists, trying to ward off the crushing pang my sister's words kick up.

"But I bet she'd try to distract me, you know? Do her Lucille Ball impression or something, and she would stay, I'm sure of it, even if she just got in everybody else's way. Bri, she'd drive the nurses nuts!"

"She would!" We both break out laughing. "And she wouldn't even care."

"Not one bit." Missy settles, staring down at her lap. "You know what I hate?"

"What?"

"The word slut." She looks back up, eyeing me, perhaps to get a feel for what I think, to sense, through my expression, if I recognize her in the word... in its meaning.

"I don't like it either. It's cruel and not even that descriptive."

"They call me that, you know."

"Who?" I prod, placing my hand on Missy's knee. "Chelsea and Kayla? Scott?"

Missy flinches as I mention the last name. A rush of fury springs from my stomach like a bubbling blood fountain. I swallow, quarantine the rage, giving it room to simmer in the back of my throat.

"Everyone. The whole school. Don't you hear anything?"

I shrug. "You know I don't really talk to anyone. I mean, well, I did speak to Chelsea and Kayla, but it wasn't by choice. They kinda cornered me in the bathroom a while back, but other than that—" I decide to take the plunge. "Chelsea did say something to me this morning. She knows what happened last night." While I know the small fabrication isn't entirely fair to my sister – Chelsea didn't say she knew exactly what happened to Missy – I let my intuition guide me.

Grabbing my arm, Missy begins to shiver. I open my mouth to call for a nurse when she yanks my shirtsleeve hard enough for me to let out a yelp. "Bri, don't say anything! Don't you say a word! You got me?"

"Just tell them!" I stand, my chest heaving. I cover my face with both hands.

"You can't say anything, Bri! I'll die if you do. I… I'll kill myself."

Letting my arms drop, I stare open-mouthed. An image of Dad veering off into the wrong lane, his eyes filled with terror for those few seconds, those last seconds before the crash, hover before me. As if she can read me, seeing exactly what I see, my image of the real-life scene that branded us, left a forever mark on our childhood, Missy nods, her face cold, completely still.

"I—" I begin when a woman in turquoise bursts through the door. She doesn't even bother to knock.

As I leave Missy grumbling to the nurse about having to take two caterpillar-sized pills, Missy calls to me. "Bri, not a word."

I shake my head, thrust open the door and dash down the hall. All I want is Cameron, to see him, to get out of this blinding home for the sick.

~ ~ ~ ~

The doorman waves, winking at me as I follow Cameron to the elevator. My eyes, itchy from crying the entire walk from the hospital to Cameron's apartment building, look more like veiny fireballs than anything human as I inspect them in the elevator mirror. I could be a creature from one of those low-budget sci-fi movies Missy and I would watch late at night when neither of us could sleep.

Cameron puts his hand on my shoulder. "You still look beautiful," he whispers. His hushed voice soothes me like the song Dad used to sing when Missy and I were little – the one about the cat and the cradle. Our eyes meet in the mirror and I turn, facing him directly. I put my arms around his thick chest and when the sliding door opens, he leads me to the small apartment he shares with his dad.

"Will he mind?" I ask as Cameron unlocks the front door. "Your dad, I mean. You're sure he won't be mad about you bringing a girl home?"

"Doubt it, but he's working late, anyways. Plus Dad's a pretty chill guy. You'd like him."

Cameron's bedroom is painted a light blue. Something about the color makes me think of little kids playing with toy sailboats – Cameron, age four: I can see him scuttling around the giant pond in Central Park, a shoe-sized wooden boat clutched in his chubby hands.

"Who's that?" I point to a picture on his desk. The woman – whispy brown hair, jeans and an oversized white t-shirt – grins, posing hand-on-hip for the camera.

"My mom." Cameron lifts the silver frame, handing it over.

I run my index finger over the photograph. "She's pretty."

"That was taken before I was born. In fact, she may have been a little pregnant there, though, of course, you can't tell."

"You really miss her." I place the picture back in its spot.

"She made her choice. It was a free life, no big responsibilities or us, her family. She made the selfish choice. I miss when she was around, when she played my mom, but sometimes I think that was just an act, a part she played because it seemed like the thing she was supposed to do."

"Well, it's her loss." The words feel awkward, unrehearsed coming out – *Her loss*, because it isn't really her loss; it's everyone's... the entire family's loss. I think about my mom. If she were running around Pennsylvania, getting her hair and nails done once a week, going on daily shopping sprees, I'd hate her for it. Something tells me she's not having the time of her life, that, wherever she is, the problems she's carried for almost forty-six years are trailing her, wearing her thin.

Plopping down on Cameron's bed, the mattress feels warm, comforting as it bears my weight. I motion toward a poster on the wall. It's one of the few decorations in Cameron's sparse, seemingly unclaimed room. *No Direction Home: Bob Dylan*. A man dressed all in black, his hands in his pockets, stands before a country road.

"You like Dylan?" Cameron joins me on the bed.

"I just know the tambourine song. Dad used to sing

it to us when we were little. He sang to us every night."

"To me he's the greatest. No one compares, not even The Beatles."

No direction home. I lay down, feet dangling off the side of the bed. *No direction home*, perhaps because there is no home, no place to be directed to.

"So…" Cameron scooches closer, brushing my arm with his knuckles. "I don't know when my dad will be back. He sometimes works till three AM. I can just go into the living room if you want to get some rest here. The couch is comfortable and—"

"Can you explain something to me?" I turn onto my side, my nose only a few inches from Cameron's. His breath is warm. I can almost taste the salt from his mouth. "Why do so many men want to hurt women?"

"God, Bri." Cameron looks up at the ceiling for a moment. "I don't know. I guess… I guess it's because they're insecure. I can't think of any other explanation. I mean, just look at Stanley in *Streetcar*. He gets drunk then beats Stella, throws shit around, acts like an animal, but afterward he feels guilty. He thinks he's all powerful and macho but in the end, he's just an insecure guy – a big baby, really."

"But I mean…" Sitting up, I look down at Cameron's face. His averted eyes and pouting chin make my chest feel heavy. It's as though he feels responsible for the pain inflicted upon Missy, Stella, and every other girl who's suffered at the hands of a violent man. "Well…" I feel my cheeks heating up, but I ask all the same. "What is sex, then? I mean, I know how it's done; it's just, if it's not about power then… well, then I guess… is it? Maybe, I think that's my question. Is sex about power?"

"Not at all!" Cameron sits up, his eyes perfectly level with mine. "No! Not if it's real. Real sex is about love."

An image of Jim flickers before me. In his boxers and torn undershirt, he ambles down the stairs and into the kitchen, a smirk like a trail of slug scum smeared across his lips. He grabs a beer then settles in front of the TV, his legs wide open.

"Hey, can you get me one of those?" Mom appears on the landing. She smoothes her crinkled nightgown.

"Get your own," Jim snaps, not even bothering to look up.

I stare at the open bedroom door then back at Cameron. The memory of Jim has passed on, been buried. I offer a swift nod of my head in place of a prayer. Rising slowly, I walk over and shut the door.

Chapter Thirteen

Crocuses poke through moist dirt, their colorful, brave heads testing the late April air. Rounding the corner, I stop to inspect a boxed-in patch, a typical city street garden that will soon be filled with spring flowers. I realize, reaching down to brush my fingers over the largest of the bunch, the almost-flower that will soon tower over its family, a radiant big sister, her purple arms ready to embrace the coming season, that it's been over a month since my name appeared on the spring play cast list: *Sabrina Gibbons to play Stella in* A Streetcar Named Desire. It's been over a month since Missy came home from the hospital plagued by constant nightmares, and over a month since Cameron taught me what love in its most physical form should feel like.

Passing Scott Shapiro as I hurry down the lobby hallway and toward the elevator – play practice set to begin in five minutes – I stop, narrow my eyes and leer. He looks away, as he always does, but he knows. He knows I know what he did to my sister and, relying on the information Ms Rourke from the Special Victims Unit gave Grandma, Grandpa and me, I know his days as a free man are numbered.

"When a victim decides to speak out," Ms Rourke explained, "she takes that crucial step away from being a victim, towards becoming a survivor. Give Marissa time. It will happen."

The chatter comes to a halt as I burst through the theater doors. Skylar and Aaron sit at the edge of the stage, Cameron standing in front of them. "What?" I raise my arms. the sudden silence feels like an insult. "I'm not late. It's only—"

"Did you turn your phone off, Bri?" Cameron walks toward me, his cell in his hand.

"I don't—" I reach into my knapsack, fumbling around for the gift Grandma gave me for my birthday. "I don't know if I... I may have left it in the park. Damn it! I was down by the river and—"

Cameron thrusts his phone to my ear. Grandma's frantic voice cracks as I try to listen to the message on Cameron's voicemail. I worry about her – her heavy breathing and rapid speech. "You need to come home" is all I make out before running back out of the theater.

"Do you want me to come?" Cameron calls out. I don't respond.

My grandparents' front door rests open on its hinges. I enter, my heart sputtering like an old car. A whiff of lilac strikes me first, pungent and over-applied. I tiptoe to the coat rack, following the scent, and, as my hand brushes that leopard print fur coat I'd recognize almost as well as my own reflection, I hear a gasp.

Her eyes, two shimmering black globes, wide-open, healthy and fresh, Mom throws her arms out. At this moment, I am not the mature seventeen-year-old, the young woman who already understands what's most important in life – love, friendship, connection and commitment. I'm the child, the chubby-fingered six-year-old barely able to contain her excitement as her mother appears, stage right, in full command of the room's attention.

"Bear! My Bri-bear!" Mom places her hands on my shoulders, stepping back from a caress I've longed for these past three months. She looks me up and down. "I'd almost forgotten." She covers her mouth, turning back to look at Grandma. "I'd almost forgotten what a beauty my first baby is."

Her face drawn, eyes facing downward, Grandma stands with her shoulder pressed against the kitchen door. "A lot has happened since you've been gone." Grandma turns, pushing the door open. "You've missed an awful lot."

"Well, I'm here now! Come," Mom grabs me by the arm. "Let's go into my old room. You can tell me everything you've been up to! We'll leave the old folks to do their thing."

Halfway down the hall, I turn back. Grandma has disappeared into the kitchen. I hear her and Grandpa's muffled voices.

~ ~ ~ ~

As though it had been ages since she last saw the room, Mom inspects every crevice, letting out exclamations of wonderment. In a tight black top, fitted jeans and leather boots, her hair colored a dark brown –

almost black – and carefully shaped and blow-dried, she looks like a woman who hasn't a care in the world; nothing but her appearance to look after.

"Where were you?" I settle on the bed. Looking down at my washed jeans, my tennis shoes, wisps of split ends falling past my shoulders, I feel frumpy for the first time in months – uncomfortable in my own skin.

"Around." She points to my bulletin board. "You took down the poster."

"It's in the closet," I shrug.

Walking up to the board, she presses her finger against the old photo of herself. "Where did you get that?" She turns sharply, her eyes wide, accusatory.

"From a box of things you threw out years ago."

"You kept it all this time?" She pulls out the tack and takes the picture in her hands.

I rush to her side, grabbing the photo. It's one of the few pieces I have to remember my father by. "If you didn't want it anymore, I—"

"You know that was with Tom when he died, don't you?"

Sticking the Polaroid back beneath Emily Dickinson's poem, I nod. "I remember when you brought it home from the hospital – Dad's wallet, his brown leather coat and this, his favorite picture of you from a trip by the seaside. There was nothing else."

Flipping her hair, Mom stares up at the ceiling. "There's something, oh… unnecessary about drudging up the past. You know what I mean?" She folds her arms, eyeing me. "It's done with, old news; that's why time goes forward, not backwards – never backwards."

"Isn't that why memories are so important?" As the

words form, sliding without a tinge of difficulty from my lips, I realize this is the first time I have ever challenged my mother. I take it one step further. "I don't think you're right. I think the past is very important to keep in mind. How else would people learn? We need the past to have experience."

Before Mom can respond, though by the flush of her cheeks I can tell she's taken aback, there's a knock on the door. Turning the knob, Grandma stands still in the entryway, Missy on one side, Grace on the other. Mom rushes to my sisters when, to my surprise, Grace begins to sob. She grabs Grandma's arm, pulling her back, away from the door.

"What is this?" Grandma scolds, practically falling over. "What's this nonsense? Go! Say hello to your mother!"

"Out!" Grace screams. "Out! Out!"

"What have you done?" Mom starts toward Grandma. "Grace," she orders. "Come here!"

Grace shakes her head, her hands on her hips. Leering, she reaches up and dries her cheeks. "Go home!"

Missy springs to my side, taking my hand.

"You did this!" Mom shoves her finger in Grandma's face. "You! You poisoned my children against me."

"No!" Grandma snaps, her eyes flaming circles of steady oak. "You did this one, Sheila. This was your mistake."

Mom turns, her cheeks smeared with water and make-up. I hadn't even noticed she was crying. "Come," she beckons, facing Missy and me. "You two come. Grace will follow. I have the rental car outside.

It's due back in Butler tonight."

Her head down, Missy takes a step forward. I yank her back. "Not now. We can't now, Momma."

"Sabrina. I—" Mom's voice breaks. "I need you. I mean all three of you." She turns to Missy, swivels around to see Grace. "Bear, I don't want to live away from you."

I look to Missy for strength, desperately avoiding my mother's pleading stare.

"You could stay here." Missy squeezes my hand tighter then adds the other for support. "It would be like all the times before. You could have your old room back. Bri and I don't mind doubling up."

With a sigh, Mom takes my hand and Missy's. She kisses us both on the forehead.

"Come. I can't offer all this." Spinning on her heals, she gestures toward the sturdy walls, the high ceiling that doesn't shed paint chips every time a door slams shut. "But what does that matter? You don't need this, right?"

I shake my head, my eyes level with hers. "We want to stay. We have to. Our lives are here now."

"Okay. Okay, then." Straightening her shirt, Mom takes a deep breath. "This is home." She looks past Missy and me, her gaze seemingly fixed on my bulletin board. "You've both grown so big." She smiles. "I love you, all three of you. You know that, don't you?"

I nod, a feeling of relief rippling through my tensed figure. She'll stay and it'll be like old times. I'll tell her I'm playing Stella in *Streetcar*; she can even help me with my lines! I bet she never thought she'd get a chance to read Blanche again. Grace will calm down once she realizes she doesn't have to leave Grandma.

Everything will be alright.

"Where are you going?" I follow Mom as she takes her coat from the rack and heads for the front door.

"I—" She pauses, turning to face us. "I have to move the car."

"Let me come with you." I scurry to her side.

"No." She stands in the doorway. "You just stay here. I'll be back before you know it."

Fluid

Sometimes our memories are the most solid things we have to hold on to. I keep mine from those three months in 2009 in a chest, one made out of smooth, emerald green glass. It sits, undisturbed, close to the midpoint of my mind. There are days when I feel steady enough to unlatch the lid and peek through, and days when I choose to keep the box sealed. At the bottom of my chest I see a frigid winter afternoon – three lost girls roaming their grandparents' long hallway waiting for their mother to come through the front door. At the top, just beneath the glass dome cover, there is an image of all five of us, Grandma, Grandpa, Missy, Grace and me. We stand still at our front door, taking in the news, each trying to hold on, keep sturdy for the others.

When my mother stepped on the pedal, veering off halfway across the George Washington Bridge, only stone and metal between her and the Hudson, she took two lives; at least that's how I see it. There was the past, a full-figured container of history, feelings and memories, most of which caused her great suffering, but there was also a future, an unfertilized, yet ever-ready-to-sprout seed of hope. Both slid away that afternoon in late April.

The Hungarians have a word, *balsors*, which literally means ill fate, though it is sometimes translated as misfortune. Unlike misfortune, balsors is a burden that generally lasts a lifetime because fate can never be changed. Grandma and Grandpa believed that Mom's death was another blow dealt by God, the same almighty being who, in spite of hours of prayer and a mass of sacrificed possessions, took the lives of Grandma's two brothers and my father, who allowed Missy to be raped at fifteen, and who was responsible for the failure of the Hungarian Revolution of 1956. We knew better.

After Mom's death, Missy, Grace and I made a pact. Life, as we already knew, is a fluid tale – ups, downs, moments of being ambushed, splashed against the side without the slightest hint of what to expect – but in spite of our pasts, turbulent as they were, the three of us made a promise to go forward with hope and fearlessness.

Missy kept her promise one morning in mid-May. With Ms Rourke at her side, she showed up, walked to the front of my homeroom and pointed to three giggling teens in the back of the classroom. "Scott Shapiro," she spoke, loud and clear. "He's the one who raped me, beating me when I tried to fight back, and those two, Chelsea and Kayla, watched. They watched and laughed the whole time."

Five years later, Grace got up from the kitchen table, my old copy of *Jane Eyre* in her hand as she held the portable phone in place with her skinny shoulder. Missy and I watched as she spoke to Jim for the first time since we left Butler. She took down his new address, some place in Ohio, and couldn't have managed more than a dozen words before Grandma barged in, insisting she hand over the phone. "Don't you dare call here again," Grandma roared, slamming down the receiver. That night Grace sat with me in my bedroom and wrote a letter.

Dear Dad,

I am sorry to hear that you are sick and can't work anymore. Here is $150. It's all I have saved up. Please don't call me again. I don't want to be mean, I just don't think I want to know you anymore. I hope you understand.

Grace

I guess that brings us to me. I played Stella all those years ago. I haven't acted since, but whenever *A Streetcar Named Desire* is performed anywhere nearby, or the film version is on late at night, I get a little tug in the pit of my stomach. These days I'm working towards a Masters degree in Social Work. I'd like to work with people who suffer from Bipolar Disorder – at least that's the plan for now, but as we all know, plans change. You may be wondering what happened with Cameron. Well, guess what? I married him.

The End

ABOUT THE AUTHOR

Emma Eden Ramos is a writer from New York City. Her middle grade novella, *The Realm of the Lost*, was published in 2012 by MuseItUp Publishing. Her short stories have appeared in *Stories for Children Magazine, The Storyteller Tymes, BlazeVOX Journal*, and other journals. Ramos' novelette, *Where the Children Play*, is included in *Resilience: Stories, Poems, Essays, Words for LGBT Teens*, edited by Eric Nguyen. *Three Women: A Poetic Triptych and Selected Poems* (Heavy Hands Ink, 2011), Ramos' first poetry chapbook, was shortlisted for the 2011 Independent Literary Award in Poetry. Emma studies psychology at Marymount Manhattan College. When she isn't writing, Emma can usually be found drinking green tea and reading on her kindle.

18189000R00079

Made in the USA
San Bernardino, CA
03 January 2015